CAPTIVE OF DESIRE

BEAUTIFUL DECEIT SERIES
BOOK TWO

FELICITY BRANDON

FREE SEXY READS

Sign up for my newsletter and receive FREE sexy reads
here!
https://felicitybrandonwrites.com/newsletter/

PROLOGUE: KADE WALKER

Growing orchids taught me about the value of patience. If you wanted the flowers to bloom, you had to wait. You had to be diligent, deliver everything the plant needed, nurture its growth, and provide the perfect conditions. You couldn't rush the process. It couldn't be accelerated. The orchid blossomed in its own sweet time.

Looking back, I wished I'd cultivated them from a younger age. How many of the women I'd taken and slain would have survived if I had only applied the orchid's rules? Running my fingertips over Tiffany's soft skin, I blew out a breath at the litany of terrible, sordid memories. The list of lives I had snuffed out was longer than I wanted to remember.

As a younger man, I'd been heady with power, with little desire to nurture anything except my satisfaction. Tiffany was the first I yearned to look after, the first I'd chosen to flourish at my fingertips.

"It's okay," I whispered, relishing her tiny whimpers. "You're safe."

Though safety, I realized, was a relative concept. She may

well have expected to be safe in her own home, but I had infested it and changed all the rules. Now, Tiffany's safety relied upon her ability to please me. Now, everything was different.

Wide eyes met my assertion, her lips struggling around the gag I'd shoved into place. Forced onto her belly, her ankles and wrists were bound with the same black ropes I'd used before.

"It's necessary." I met her gaze, ensuring she understood before I rose from her easy chair.

"I'll be back soon. Then we'll talk more, and you can send your message to your boss." I resisted the urge to roll my eyes, although I desperately wanted to. Tiffany's obsession with her career was one fetish I intended to suppress. A woman as wonderful as her deserved a life of sensuality and pleasure, not heavy caseloads and courtrooms. I would give her life the meaning she'd so frantically sought but failed to find.

Her breathing was ragged as I stalked away, heading out to the landing. Following the blood stains, my gaze landed on the place she'd flung the bloodied knife, and my fingers rose to the dressing at my neck. A part of me still couldn't believe she had attacked me, that she loathed me so intensely, violence with a knife had seemed like a good plan. Glancing back, I caught her despairing expression, my arousal simmering as she squirmed in the ropes. Technically, the spreader bar at her ankles meant she hadn't needed binding there, but I'd been having too much fun to stop. Instead, I'd wound the rope around every limb, ensuring she was thoroughly fettered and adequately photographed. Even though I had cameras littered all around the place, I intended to keep a thorough record of her struggles with the images captured on my phone, so I could relish Tiffany's plight whenever the urge struck.

Ignoring my burgeoning need, I headed down the hall to the house's main bathroom, where Tiffany kept an extensive first aid kit. Away from her distracting mewls, I could give the laceration some proper attention. Finding the kit under the basin, I watched in the mirror as I peeled away the dressing. The bleeding had stopped, but it was vulnerable to infection. God only knew how long she'd kept the blade by her bedside, but its condition had hardly been sterile. I found antiseptic cream and applied a thin layer to the wound before putting on a fresh dressing. Hopefully, that would suffice and keep infection at bay. The last thing I needed was to fall foul of its symptoms. I finally had everything I wanted and refused to permit illness to rain on my parade.

Tidying up, I closed the kit and caught sight of my reflection in the bathroom cabinet. The gray eyes that had haunted me looked brighter in the morning sunshine as if Tiffany had injected them with hope. My lips curled. That was precisely what she had done. She didn't know it, but the woman had become my reason for living—the very essence of who I was. Having her to cherish had turned my life around, and the bloodlust I used to enjoy was a thing of the past. Hell, I hadn't even retaliated after she'd cut me. I was a far cry from the monster I once was.

Turning over a new leaf didn't mean there wouldn't be consequences, though. I'd already told Tiffany, once our immediate needs had been met, she would pay the price for her insolence and had already conceived the perfect punishment. Fortunately for her, I had no desire to play with knives and had resolved to never cause her actual harm, but that didn't mean I would go easy on her. The writhing little brunette would soon realize there were repercussions for her actions. I'd hidden away in the attic long enough. Her master was here to steer her on this journey of submission—whether or not she liked it.

Striding back to the bedroom, I stood in the doorway, surveying her. Catching sight of me, she froze, her fingers splayed as she presumably tried to decide on my mood.

"How are you doing, little girl?" I crossed the room to where she was sprawled, falling to my haunches to address her. "Have you been good?"

She nodded emphatically, apparently keen to persuade me of her obedience.

"Good."

I smoothed her hair from her face, trying not to be diverted by her delicious form. Being around a naked-and-bound Tiffany was like a perpetual hard-on, a fervor I'd have to learn to control if I wanted this flower to bloom.

"Because we have things to do."

CHAPTER 1: TIFFANY NOBLE

Hand trembling, I took the phone from him and accessed my contacts. Yesterday, I'd handled the device with swift dexterity, not giving its use a second thought, but today, everything was different. With Kade towering over me—the power of his stare burning into my face and the memory of how he'd had me bound, only moments before, fresh in my mind—I could barely keep the mobile steady.

"Remember what I told you." His voice was little more than a snarl.

"Yes, Master." Swallowing back rising nausea, I tried to focus.

"Any funny business and I'll have you bound permanently. I'm more than capable of messaging on your behalf."

The knot of anxiety twisted in my stomach. Kade was certainly capable. He'd proven that on more than one occasion while I'd screwed up the only opportunity I'd had to be free. Struggling to catch my breath, my gaze flitted to his eyes to find his menacing gray orbs fixed on me. Biting my lip, my focus fell to the dressing on his neck, the evidence of my attack.

I'd done that.

The truth reverberated in my head. I'd cut him. Guilt knotted in my chest as I recalled slicing his throat with the knife. Clearly, I hadn't used enough force to do any lasting damage, but still, I'd wielded the blade. I'd been prepared to kill. My brow furrowed, confused by his survival. I didn't want to be a murderer, but I couldn't cope with being his captive. What was I going to do?

"What's the problem, little girl?" Kneeling in front of me, Kade folded his arms across his strapping chest, tightening the chain still attached to the collar at my neck. I lurched forward, steadying myself before I dropped my phone. "Why are you making me wait?"

"I'm sorry." I could scarcely think straight. "I don't know what to say."

"We already discussed what to say." His brows knitted, conveying his irritation as his hands reached for the screen. "Find your boss' contact."

"Yes, Master." Acting on autopilot, I searched my contacts for Rex's number, pulling it up on the screen.

"Start a new message." Kade's voice had softened as he eased behind my body and straddled my legs, still forced apart by the spreader bar at my ankles. "I'll help you." Snaking around my body, his arms grazed over my aching nipples to my hands, and God help me, I arched my back into him.

Stop that. The snarky voice in my head screamed the warning. *Stop sending him the wrong signs.*

Panting at his sudden proximity, it was already too late. I'd ceded to his desire, willingly taking his enormous cock when he'd claimed me and—to my shame—loved every moment of his possession. I loathed the things Kade stood for, despised what he'd done, but when push came to shove, the man knew how to play my body like an instrument. He owned me in a way no one else had ever achieved. My head spun at the disturbing realization.

Kade had screwed me, and I'd adored it. I should have been worried about the unprotected sex, should have a head filled with fear about sexually transmitted infections and pregnancy, should have been disgusted and outraged. *Why wasn't I?* He'd bound, plugged, and demeaned me, and instead of shriveling in fear, I'd bloomed. What the hell was wrong with me?

"How would you start a message to him?" Kade whispered the question into my nape, sending electricity sparking along my spine.

"H-Hi, Rex." I struggled to get the words out.

"Go ahead then." The hand stroking my wrist gestured for me to act, and gripping the device, I typed.

Hi, Rex,

"Tell him you're ill," Kade purred. "That you've been up all night vomiting."

"O-Okay."

Sorry, I can't come to the office today. I've been ill all night and am still vomiting this morning.

"Very good."

I could hear the smile on his lips, the sound unexpectedly soothing.

"That should buy us the rest of the day, at least."

"What happens after that, Master?" I turned toward him, our gazes locking.

"You let me worry about those details." His silver gaze was cold. "Remember?"

"Yes."

Kade made everything sound so simple. Rex was my boss, the man who held my career aspirations in the palm of his hand. I didn't like lying to him any more than I liked being held under duress. Pulling in a shaky breath, I grappled with the trepidation churning in my belly.

"How would you sign off the message?"

Kade's right hand brushed past my breast. Attention lowered, I watched as my flesh goosed, my nipple beading into a tight bud. It didn't seem to matter the man had taken and tormented me, that he had no right to be there, to be doing the things he was doing—my body responded to him as if the title he insisted I use was correct. It recognized my master.

I'll be in touch,

Tiff

I held my breath as I finished, waiting on Kade's verdict.

"Tiff?" He snorted. "Is that what he calls you?"

"It's what most people call me, Master."

"But why? Tiffany is a lovely name."

He snuggled closer, pressing the denim of his pants against my tender ass. Clenching around the butt plug still lodged inside me, my throat dried. I didn't like the ruthless side of Kade, but this quiet attempt at affection was just as perturbing. I never knew what was going to come next. "

"I-I don't know." I had no answers for him. I'd been known as Tiff for as long as I could recall.

"Just as well you're my little girl, then." His breath was hot against my neck. My eyes fluttered closed as his lips brushed over my sensitive skin. "That's all I'll ever need to call you."

"Why, Master?" I croaked, conscious of how horny his show of authority was making me. My fingers tightened around my phone as if their plan was to use the device as a weapon, but I knew better. I'd wielded a much more impressive weapon and failed to achieve my aim—probably because I didn't truly know what my aim was. I wanted to be free of Kade's aggressive possession but couldn't imagine another day without it.

It didn't make sense that his predatory tenderness should be so alluring, especially since I'd lived through a couple of his trials and understood precisely what an ordeal they were, but there was little point in denying the way he affected me. Kade had discovered it for himself, especially when he'd buried his satisfying shaft inside my wet, demanding pussy. Once more, my muscles clenched at the memory.

"Why what?"

"Why am I your *little girl?*" My eyes flickered open to find him right there, his dark eyebrow arched as if he was daring me to defy him.

"Because I like it." His lips curled. "You like it, too, don't you?"

Did I?

My lips parted as though the answer would come automatically, but I didn't have a response. I'd never known 'little girl' to be used sexually before Kade smashed into my life, but he had a way of making the innocuous sound sinful and dirty.

"I don't know, Master."

"Well, I do." He pinched my nipple casually, then cradled my breast as his other hand slipped between my legs. Balanced on my knees with my ankles forced apart, there was little to prevent his exploration. "Drop your phone, little girl."

The device slipped from my fingers, falling to the carpet below.

"Very good." His patronizing tone should have irked, but I was so caught in the rapture of his fingers as they brushed over my clit and skimmed my swollen labia, I couldn't think, let alone contemplate the offense. "Slide your hands down by your thighs and keep them there."

I complied, feeling his arms tighten around me as soon as my palms rested against my legs.

"I still have to send the message, Master," I reminded him, the final fragments of my independent mind desperate to salvage whatever was left of my professional reputation. I'd never missed a day of work before, had never so much as taken a sick day, and the seven missed calls from my office were a testament to that fact.

"I know." His voice vibrated past me as his fingertips parted my lips and pushed lightly into my pussy. "We'll send it soon."

"Oh God," I gasped, my head rolling back against him as he filled me with one, then two digits. I wanted him so much, wanted him to take control and own me as he'd done before. At that moment, kneeling there, I no longer cared if it made sense. I only knew this was the culmination of a lifetime of unfulfilled longing.

"Exactly." His tone had grown husky. "First, I remind you what happens to good little girls, then once we're both gratified, you'll send your message."

CHAPTER 2: KADE

Spent with lust, I folded over her diminutive body. It was true then—the first time with Tiffany had not been a fluke. She was as sweet, as wet, and as responsive as I remembered. Grinning, I nuzzled her nape, reveling in her throaty moans. She looked hotter than hell with a gag in place, but there was nothing quite like the soundtrack of her sensation to spiral my passion to the sky.

"That's better." I kissed her, meandering an arm around her chest to draw her back to her knees. "Isn't it, little girl?"

"Yes, Master." There was no hesitation, her sex clenching around my shaft where we were still joined.

I took a moment to breathe in all that I'd achieved—her captivity and the start of her conditioning, but more than that, the hedonistic bliss we'd conjured. Aside from her unhinged attack, everything had gone better than I could have hoped, and the best was yet to come.

"I love being inside you." There was no harm in relaying my feelings. I was certain my enthusiastic cock had already conveyed most of the message. "Sadly, there are other things we must do." I withdrew, immediately rueful at the loss of intimacy.

"Master?" She twisted, trying to catch my eyes.

Anxiety danced in her blue gaze, reminding me of the most gratifying facet of our union—only *I* knew what would come next.

"Hush." I met her eyes, my attention settling on her. "Remember what we discussed?"

She nodded, her focus falling back to the floor as she mumbled her acquiescence.

"Tell me." Rising above her, I pulled up and zipped my pants.

"I'm to obey you." Her shoulders rose, the tension seeping into them clear to see. I would need to ease that strain away in the future, to lay my hands on her and persuade the stiffness from her aching muscles—but that time was not now. This moment, and the proceeding ones, were about penance —about Tiffany making amends for her knife play.

"That's right." I ruffled her hair and circled her body, smiling at her vexed expression. Soon, she would have too many other things to concern herself with. Her hair would be the least of her worries.

"We're going back to the attic."

Her breath caught. "But, why, Mast—" Her sentence halted as she caught sight of my unimpressed gaze.

"Better," I praised, though my tone still spoke of the ramifications to come. "Don't forget your place, little girl."

Her furrowing brow was the only evidence of her disquiet.

"Come on." Reaching forward, I hiked her to her feet. "Much though it would be fun to see you attempt to walk there, it will be faster if I give you a lift." Grabbing her hips, I threw her over my shoulder, her frantic yelp ringing in my ear as I stalked from the bedroom. I held on to her fabulous ass as I took the steps two at a time, squeezing the orbs and nudging the plug before striding to the attic. Placing her back on her feet, I helped her to her knees.

"Face the wall." Kind master that I was, I'd set up the training equipment in the carpeted part of the attic. She eyed the contraption, rightly nervous about the six inches of plastic she found protruding from the wall.

"Know what that is?" I arched a brow.

"N-No, Master."

"Are you sure about that?" I prompted, smiling at her feigned innocence. "Haven't you seen something similar online?"

Her face blanched as she glanced back at the black plastic. "I…" Panic flashed in her eyes as she turned back to me.

"Is that a yes?" I couldn't deny how much I thrived on her fright. I'd always intended to use the apparatus on my little girl, but her violence had gifted me an unexpected justification. Nothing I did to her now—short of my own uncontrolled aggression—could be seen as unwarranted after she'd slashed me.

"Yes, Master." She pulled in a shaky breath, her gaze falling to her knees.

"Then you know what it's for." I motioned toward it. "Crawl closer." Folding my arms across my chest, I waited as she shuffled nearer. It was obvious that every fiber of her being wanted to resist, but we both knew she had no choice. Her surrender would be all the sweeter now that it was masked as redemption from her sins.

"You'll notice we're starting with the beginner dildo." I moved closer, idly running a finger over the rigid plastic. "Only six inches."

"It's huge, Master." She swallowed, her chest rising and

falling as she took in what those full six inches would mean for her throat.

"Nonsense." I laughed at her terror, flourishing as she squirmed. Her fate was inevitable, and watching the realization on her face was better than I could ever have imagined. "I'm much bigger, and you managed me just fine." My lips curled at the mesmerizing memory.

"But you're not so unyielding, Master."

My brow rose at her unlikely response. Of all the ways she might describe me, I hadn't expected that.

"I am the reward you get for being a good girl," I reminded her, wandering behind her body and wrapping my hand around her nape. "When you came at me with a knife, you forfeited that right."

"I..." Once again, she considered trying to justify her behavior but wisely gave up the pursuit.

"Exactly."

Her silence spoke volumes. Tiffany deserved this punishment, and she knew it.

"I have an eight-inch version as well." My fingers tightened at the back of her neck. "And one that measures ten inches."

She gasped, surveying the mere six inches in front of her.

"You can consider this starter dick as charity and thank me for my compassion."

"Th-Thank you, Master." She tried to pull away, but my hand held her steady.

"You're welcome, little girl. Just so we're clear about my expectations, this device will serve as your penance, as well as part of your training. Your throat is divine, but we need to work on that gag reflex. This will help you."

"But I won't be able to breathe! I'll—"

Reaching down, I swatted her exposed backside, the sting ending her futile complaint.

"You can breathe just fine," I reassured. "Your nose will be unhindered throughout."

"Master, please."

Her desperation was so fucking sexy. I wished I could indulge her plea and have her then and there, but that was not what this was about.

"You can show me gratitude later." I straightened, keeping the pressure at her nape. "First, it's punishment time."

"How long do I have to stay there?" Her gaze darted to mine.

"You stay on the dildo as long as I tell you." My cock swelled at the wonderful prospect. "The more fuss you make, the longer it's likely to be."

Reaching into my pocket, I yanked out a length of rope and crouched to secure her wrists loosely behind her. Tiffany's brows knitted as she bit down on her lip, perhaps to prevent another misjudged communication.

"Come on now." I signaled for her to move forward. "Wrap your lips around it. The sooner we start, the sooner you'll be through."

And the sooner, I'll be horny enough to screw you again. I resisted the urge to vocalize the last sentence.

"Oh God." Her words were barely a whisper.

"All delays will be met with fresh spanking," I warned. "While you're attached to the contraption."

She shuffled forward as her lips parted. Watching her submit to the unforgiving device was easily one of the best moments of my life.

"Very good," I enthused, smiling at her tentative approach. "You know how this works. You'll be attached with straps, and the only way to ease the tension in the springs is to allow the plastic dick all the way down your throat." My balls tightened, recalling how good she'd felt when I'd fucked her face that way. She'd be even better after the benefit of this equipment.

"Oooh," she whimpered as I gently pushed her down the plastic shaft to fasten the strap. Once in place, she pulled against its confines, easing the strain on her throat and using her strength to keep the invader at bay. The best of it was, even at her full resistance, the dildo still penetrated her lips by a couple of inches, so she was never free of its intrusion.

"Beautiful," I cooed, shifting my hard length in my pants as I took in the look of her plight. Arms bound and still strapped into the spreader bar, there was literally nothing Tiffany could do to resist the plastic. Her struggle was all the sexier as her muscles tired and she was forced to take all six inches.

Pulling out my phone, I hit record, reveling in her fight. Once more, she pulled away, able to maintain the easier position for her throat until her muscles tired. My cock pulsed as she gave way, the plastic filling her until she gagged around it.

"Don't forget why you're there," I prompted, moving closer to capture the look of her tearing eyes. "This is a punishment, little girl, and I want you to remember the lesson.

"If you hurt me, I'll make you pay."

CHAPTER 3: TIFFANY

Panic flooded my brain, a fresh surge of frantic energy rising every time I grappled with the plastic. Pulling in air through my nostrils, I yanked my head back as far as my aching neck would allow, permitting the back of my throat a well-earned rest, although I already knew the effort was futile. The respite wouldn't last. It was as inevitable as the tide washing to shore—my muscles would scream for relief and send the dildo delving straight back to my tonsils. I had no idea how long I'd been strapped to the cruel device, but it seemed like forever. The intensity of my predicament heightened every time the plastic intruder invaded my throat again.

"Uck." I struggled around the dildo, yanking at the ropes holding my wrists together. If only I could free my hands, I could loosen the strap on my head and get this damn thing out of my mouth. If only I could relieve the pressure on my knees as I desperately tried to find a way out of this purgatory. If only…

"Stop fighting." Kade's laughter drifted past me.

Forcing my gaze in his direction, he was once again video

recording my utter degradation. I thrashed against the plastic in my mouth, drawing back again in protest, but no matter how hard I pulled, I couldn't remove the blasted thing from my mouth. Forced to endure it, I panted around its girth, my cheeks flaming as he moved the camera closer.

"Not only will it teach you a necessary lesson, but it'll train your gag reflex." He smiled as if he was doing me a favor. "You'll come to appreciate the help, little girl."

Appreciate it? The man was truly insane. How could he possibly think I would ever find value in this humiliating experience? Even as my questions pinballed in my mind, I was aware of the other no-doubt intended consequence. My body thrummed with desire for the denigration, and I knew if he reached between my legs, he'd find me soaking—not only from the orgasm he'd granted in my bedroom—but from this new sordid nightmare.

It made no sense to be allured by such flagrant struggling, but I had to admit it—if only to myself—it turned me on. That's why I'd watched content that featured similar devices, why I'd used vibrators to increase my pleasure as I imagined being used this way. As with so many of these experiences, though, the reality was far more intense than I could ever have dreamed.

I groaned as my weary neck compelled me back down the plastic shaft, choking around the tip as it grazed the back of my throat. It was crazy enough that anything about this was arousing, but surely, he couldn't intend to keep me this way for long? I'd go mad, caught in the conflict between blowing the dildo and enduring the tension in my neck.

"Very nice." Kade slid his phone away, unzipped his pants, and took his swollen erection in his fist. "It's a shame I removed those lovely clamps, but there's always next time, I suppose."

Eyeing him through wet lashes, I could barely believe what I heard. Kade had whipped the clamps from my nipples before he fucked me and finally hit send on the message to Rex, but the sensitive tissue still ached at the lingering memory. The thought of being made to endure more agony while I countered the evil contraption was too much to tolerate.

"Just as well, I can improvise." He chuckled, lowering to his knees beside me. "Isn't it, little girl?"

I whimpered around the plastic, my apprehension skyrocketing as he crawled into position behind me. Fighting against the plastic invader in my mouth, I sensed his hands rising to cradle my breasts.

"Lovely," he enthused, squeezing my mounds before his fingers splayed, tweaking my nipples between his fingers.

"Oooh," I whined, unable to resist his exploration any more than I could remove the plastic from between my lips. "Eeese."

"You want more, baby?"

I could hear the smile on his face as he intentionally misjudged my plea.

"Of course, your wish is my command." His hands shifted position, his fingers and thumbs pinching my teats and elongating them. "Gotta get these used to being clamped. I expect my property to be decorated."

Tears fell as he tweaked harder, pain spiking before morphing into sweet hedonistic glee. He knew how much I loathed the deed, but he was also aware I'd find the whole ordeal as sexy as hell.

"You are gorgeous." His words vibrated down my neck as one hand fell to my pussy. "And so fucking wet."

I closed my eyes as his fingers slipped between my lips, acknowledging he was right. For all my struggling and distress, I'd rarely been hornier. The realization was as brutal as the invading plastic.

"You really like this, huh?" For once, it wasn't conceit in his tone but something that sounded close to awe.

"Oh od."

He was right. The worst of it was, I couldn't deny what was so patently true.

"Hey." Kade's voice was soft. "Don't beat yourself up. I'm thrilled you enjoy this, even though it *is* supposed to be a punishment."

His words jarred in my head. It *was* a punishment—hideous, cruel, and relentless—so why was I so fucking aroused?

Gasping around the plastic, my head throbbed as if it was going to implode. I wanted to beg him for mercy, but even if I could, I didn't know what I was pleading for. Did I want to spit out the awful plastic, or could I accept the inevitability of Kade's words—that I craved this, that I'd never been so wanton?

"You are impossible to punish." His chuckle resounded past my ear as his fingertip circled my clit. "I know what you deserve, but once I get my hands on you, it's difficult to remember why it's so important."

I whimpered, caught in the frenzy of both his touch and words. I needed him to caress and careen me toward the stars, yet at the same time, I never wanted to see him again, or if I did, I wanted it to be locked in some godforsaken prison. That's what he deserved for breaking into my house and recording me. That's what this invasion warranted.

"Wait there."

I groaned as he rose to his full height, bereft at the loss of his touch, even though I had no right to be. Giving in to the screaming tension that had built up in my neck and shoulders, I relaxed, allowing the shaft back down my throat. I was getting too tired to fight, but that didn't mean I was used to the unyielding tip brushing past my tonsils. I didn't care what he said—I would never acclimatize to the gagging sensation.

"Since you've suffered so sweetly, I'm inclined to reward you."

My brows knitted at his voice, his tone smoother and more seductive. He walked behind me, towering over me as I grappled with the dildo.

"Not that you merit it, of course." He laughed softly as he settled between my legs. "But God knows, I have something of a fetish for you, little girl." He edged closer, the fabric of his pants grazing my backside as his hands slid around my thighs. "We're going to train that gag reflex, but that doesn't mean it all has to be an ordeal."

"Aster?" I wished I could turn and see his face, but the strap forcing me against the plastic meant that was impossible. The pulsing pain in my head ballooned until I couldn't decide what I was feeling anymore. Fear merged with desire to create a giddy mix of sensations.

"Shhh." He pressed his lips to the side of my neck. "You're going to work on that reflex, little girl, and I'm going to help you."

I jerked at the sound of something vibrating at my hip, panicking around the plastic as it shifted to my labia.

"I'm going to make you come while you manage the dildo." Glee oozed from his smug tone.

"Oooh," I protested, acutely conscious of the second length of plastic pressing at the apex of my thighs.

I couldn't see the device to see if it was the same vicious vibrator that had tormented me yesterday or some new acquisition, but I'd learned my lesson. Whenever Kade wielded one, it spelled trouble. This man could take pleasure and twist it into torture, but conversely, he could manifest torment into bliss.

"You're welcome." Chuckling, he pressed the pulsing plastic closer to my clit.

God help me, I welcomed the buzzing distraction. It didn't ease the pressure on my neck or in the back of my throat, but if I had to endure it—if this was my fate—then let there be pleasure as well.

"Oh!" I tipped my head back as far as the strap would permit, rocking my hips forward to increase the sweet sensation. "Oh es."

"You are a greedy girl," Kade chided, though he didn't move the vibrator. "It's just as well I'm crazy about you."

He was crazy about me?

What the hell did that mean?

I was too far down the rabbit hole to fully assess it. If his enthusiasm meant he'd let me come and take me off of this damn contraption, I'd take it and use it to my advantage.

Panting, I jerked my hips, needing more of the delicious friction. The strangest thing was, the more the heat at the core furled, the more I relaxed around the dildo in my mouth. By the time my orgasm was close, I actively worked my lips up and down the plastic as if the thing were real—a symbol of him—and I yearned to return the favor.

I detested the man but had to admit he knew how to arouse me. Kade overwhelmed me with things I'd never experienced. A part of me acknowledged that whatever happened between us—whatever my fate would ultimately be—I'd never be the same after this. Kade had changed things. He'd changed me.

"Uck." Eyes squeezed shut, I chased the climax, reveling in my subjugation. It was twisted to relish being bound and used this way. I'd never understood my proclivities but couldn't deny them.

"Come for me," Kade growled, nipping my earlobe. "Come for me, and I'll give you a reprieve from the dildo."

His words decided my plight, electricity firing between us as the first wave of desire overwhelmed me.

"That's it, little girl." His hand rose to my breasts, fondling them as I lurched with ecstasy. "You're all mine now."

CHAPTER 4: KADE

Releasing the strap, her head lolled back against my chest as though she were a rag doll. Eyes closed, drool stained her chin as I held her against me.

"Good girl," I soothed, enjoying the feel of her wonderfully firm tits as I eased her into a sitting position. She groaned as her knees were relieved of the pressure and wiggled her fingers as I settled behind her. Wrapping my arms around her, we sat together in silence.

I didn't know why I'd decided to go easy on her. When I'd secured Tiffany to the device, I'd been hellbent on making her pay, on delivering a penance she wouldn't forget, but gradually, as she grappled with the predicament, my instinct had changed. Yes, I'd adored seeing her struggle—Christ, her throaty pleas had got to me, and I was harder than I'd been for a while watching her choke around the device—but eventually, I'd softened to her mewls.

All of this had been thrust upon Tiffany in one fell swoop. Even though she'd fantasized, she'd had no time to prepare for the onslaught, no chance to ready herself for what was to come. In the end, it was that comparative innocence that saved her. Feeling her passion for me, her new fate was sealed. I would help assuage the tension tightening in her tired muscles, then elevate her back to the heavens. There would be time for training, hours to condition my little girl until she was perfect. We didn't have to achieve everything on the first day.

"Master." Her voice was hoarse as she stirred. "What just happened?"

I smiled at her innocuous question. Writhing against me, she was like a child, so small and vulnerable, and I wanted to indulge that aspect of our newfound dynamic. It hadn't been what I'd expected when I'd taken residence in the attic or what I'd anticipated as I'd plotted and planned, but holding her, it was the most natural thing in the world. She needed me, and since I'd taken her to the very brink of exhaustion, that need was now palpable. Even more bizarre, I wanted to soothe, craved the chance to cherish as well as control. Tiffany roused a need in me I hadn't known existed until this moment.

"Your punishment morphed into something sweeter." I chuckled at my own weak will, although it shouldn't have been amusing. Pressing my lips to her crown, I shook my head. What did it matter if I'd changed my mind? It altered nothing else about us. I was still in control. I would always be in control. "Did you enjoy it, little girl?"

"I hated the contraption." She practically spat out the words.

"Really?" I arched a brow. "Your pussy said otherwise."

She sighed, unable to counter my shrewd observation.

"I don't know what's wrong with me."

"There's nothing wrong with you." Tipping her head against my arm, I met her eyes, needing to reinforce this most important point. "You didn't ask to be made this way, and you're not hurting anyone by finding pleasure in it."

"You make it sound easy, Master." Her eyes flickered closed for a long moment. "It's not easy. It's far from easy."

"Nothing about you is easy." I laughed gently at my double meaning. "You're a force of nature, little girl."

"I mean it," she whispered. "I can't do this, Master. I can't live this way. I won't survive." Emotion bubbled in her voice. "Please."

"Shhh." It troubled me to see her this way, to hear her fraught resistance, but I reasoned it was inevitable. I couldn't expect to pluck her from everything she'd ever known without her opposition. Her dogged resistance, resilience, and determination were assets I most admired about the ravishing brunette.

"You'll be okay, little girl. I'll take care of you." My brow creased at the sincerity in my voice. I meant every word. I would torment and use her as it pleased me, but I fully intended to look after her, and it started today. "I'll take you to the kitchen and get you something to eat."

She shifted in my arms, glancing up at me. "You were serious about that, Master?"

"Oh, yes." I wanted to laugh at her surprise. "Deadly serious."

"O-Okay." She slumped against me, her fingers fidgeting perilously close to my crotch. Fleetingly, I was rueful to have put my cock away. "I am hungry."

"Come then." Leaping to my feet, I eased her upright. "You know the drill by now."

Her blue eyes widened as I reached for her hips, her satisfying yelp resounding around the attic space as she was flung over my shoulder. Grabbing her ass, I steadied her as I made my way down both flights of stairs into the kitchen.

"You know your way around, Master?"

"Yes, little girl." I patted her rump. "While you worked such long hours, I made myself at home." Placing her back on her feet, I steered her toward one of the stools around the grandiose marble island.

"How long were you watching me?" Her brow furrowed as she wiggled onto the seat.

She looked amazing on the stool, her legs forced apart by the spreader bar while her binds forced her arms behind her back. Her fabulous tits bounced as she tried to get comfortable—a difficult feat with her ass still full of butt plug.

"A while."

Tiffany's lips parted, though no words escaped.

"You have a lot of questions." Folding my arms across my chest, I cocked a brow at her. "Do I need to get your gag?"

"No, Master." Her reply was immediate.

"Good, because we're here to eat." I turned back to the huge refrigerator. "It's about time you ate properly." Glancing back at her stunned expression, I half expected a protest, but there was none.

"Do you like omelets, little girl?" I stared into the fridge, then grabbed the ingredients.

"I haven't had one for years, Master."

"Well, we're about to change that." I placed eggs, peppers, and onions on the counter. "They're quick, high in protein, and low in fat."

"I never thought about it." Writhing on the stool, she couldn't close her legs nor balance with her arms. Most of her weight was pushed back, driving the plug deeper into her delectable ass.

My balls tightened as my cock yearned to trade places with it. Soon, I promised myself. Stop rushing ahead. First, work on her balance. This would be a good lesson in conditioning her abs.

"But I have." I licked my lips at the delicious sight of her. As well as insisting she ate regular, healthy meals from now on, I'd also do what I could to keep her body in shape. "I told you, I intend to take care of you."

I went to work, readying the eggs and chopping the vegetables while I heated a pan. Tiffany had the advantage of a stellar and practically unused kitchen, while I had the benefit of all of those times I'd enjoyed her house in her absence. By the time I reached for two clean plates, she was shaking her head in wonder.

"Problem, little girl?" I was having fun showing off my culinary prowess. I'd always found working in the kitchen therapeutic, but having a red-hot, squirming audience was quite the aphrodisiac.

"I just can't believe this." She half-smiled. "You know your way around the entire kitchen."

"I do." I met her astonished stare as I switched off the stove. "I know lots of things about you and your life, but I want to know more." Sliding the finished omelets onto the plates, I carried them to the island, where cutlery and fresh orange juice had already been provided.

"It smells good." She breathed in the aroma, and I had to agree, my stomach growling at the scent of fried onions and peppers. "Thank you, Master."

Sliding onto the stool beside her, I smiled as I collected my cutlery.

"You're welcome."

"Er, Master?" She watched as I sliced at my omelet, enjoying the first bite.

"Hmmm?"

"How do I eat?" Her gaze fell to her sides as if I needed reminding that she was bound and helpless.

"With help." Placing down my knife and fork, I reached for hers, cutting a small piece for her. "Open wide."

Her brows knitted as she watched the fork approach her lips. "I can feed myself."

Reaching for her tantalizing right tit, I pinched her nipple. Hard.

Tiffany's eyes were like saucers as she processed the pain.

"You'll eat however I goddamn tell you to eat."

"Yes, Master."

"Eat."

I inched the fork closer, stroking the underside of her tormented breast when she finally accepted the omelet. Satisfied, I watched her chew before releasing her tit and helping myself to a second mouthful.

"That's better," I enthused, forking another bite between her lips. Eating had never been so sexy.

She perched on the stool in stunned silence, accepting piece after piece of the omelet until her plate was cleared. Once we'd both finished, I lifted her glass of orange juice to her lips, tilting it so she could drink.

"Thank you, Master." Her tone was hesitant as I placed the glass down. "I've never been fed before."

"You'll get used to it," I replied, draining the last of my juice. "At least until I can trust you, and after this,"—I gestured toward the dressing at my neck—"that won't be for some time."

Her face blanched, her gaze falling to her body as though she couldn't believe any of this had happened.

"Don't worry," I chided playfully, clearing the island. "Once you're better trained, I'll put you to work in the kitchen." I peered at her as I loaded the plates and cutlery into her dishwasher. "Maybe I'll keep you chained to the kitchen sink." I motioned toward her sparkling basin, my cock rousing at the intoxicating fantasy. "Chained, spread, and plugged."

"Master." Heat bloomed in her cheeks, suggesting she could also imagine the scenario.

"You like that?" I chuckled at her dismay. "Well, no promises, but I'll keep it in mind." Laughing, I closed the dishwasher. The two orchids I'd bought for her caught my attention. Wandering toward them, I inspected their soil before carrying them back to the island.

"They're doing much better with a little tender loving care." My statement was a thinly veiled accusation. "You never took care of them, little girl."

"I'm sorry," she gasped, her concentration flitting between staying upright on the stool, the orchids, and my face. "I didn't know how."

"You didn't know how?" I repeated skeptically. Surely, everyone knew how to nurture a plant. All it required was basic care and the right conditions.

"No, I…" Her voice trailed away. "I don't know anything about orchids."

"You could have looked up how to care for them." I pressed the point, searching her face for signs of contrition. "They were a gift, and you just let them wither."

"I was busy." Her eyes fluttered closed as though they recognized what a shit excuse that was. "I didn't think."

"That I can believe." I closed the distance between us, looming between her separated knees and compelling her eyes to open. "Now, you'll have no choice. I'll teach you how to look after them, how to help them thrive."

"Yes, Master." She craned her head to look at me. "I didn't

mean to offend you. They're just not my favorite flowers, and I—"

"Wait, what?" I interrupted. "You don't like them?" I'd never even considered Tiffany might not like orchids. Everyone loved them, didn't they? Delicate and beautiful, what wasn't to love about them?

"I like them fine." Evidently, she was struggling to appease me. "They're just not what I would have chosen for myself."

"You never bought flowers." I leaned closer. "There were never any in the house. That's why I bought some for you."

"That's true." Her breaths were coming hard and fast. "Thank you."

"So?" Reaching for her chin, I stroked her skin softly. "What flowers do you like, little girl?"

Her pupils dilated as she met my demanding gaze, and I noticed how she swallowed before she could answer.

"Chrysanthemums." Her voice was only a murmur. "I like chrysanthemums, Master."

CHAPTER 5: TIFFANY

"Really?"

Surprise glinted in his silver-gray eyes, his tone disbelieving as if he expected me to change my mind.

"Yes."

Chrysanthemums reminded me of my mother. She had grown and tended them for years before she died, and every variety of the bloom brought me back to those loaded memories, but Kade was right—I'd never contemplated buying any for myself. What would have been the point? My childhood memories were a complex myriad of happy and sad, and besides, I was never at home to enjoy flowers.

"I didn't know." He drew away as though the realization stung.

"Why would you, Master?" My brow creased as once again I acknowledged just how easy it was referring to him that way. "I rarely talk about them." I writhed on the stool, gripping the back of the seat as best I could with my bound hands. One thing was for sure, I hadn't taken into account how difficult they were to perch on without the use of your hands when I purchased them.

"Thank you for telling me."

My gaze rose to find what looked like genuine sincerity in his eyes.

"I want to know these things—what you like and don't like…" His voice dried up, somehow making the final point sound utterly salacious. "Tell me more."

"I-I don't know."

The weight of his gaze drilled into me, heating my exposed skin.

"What do you want to know, Master?"

"All of it." His gaze darkened. "What foods you love, which you abhor, which holiday destinations you still want to visit. How old were you when you first fell in love?" He shook his head, obviously frustrated. "I know so little about you."

"That's going to take a lot of time, Master."

His lips curled, lighting his face as he acknowledged my logic. I watched his expression, torn between the reality of how handsome he was and the terrible things he'd already done just by being there and treating me this way. His picture-perfect profile was difficult to reconcile with the man I'd seen in action.

"You're right, but we have time," he replied. "We have—"

His answer was cut short by the noise of a thrumming device. My belly twisting, I realized it belonged to me.

"That's my phone," I whispered, biting my lip as he reached into his pocket to retrieve it. Rex had probably replied, or maybe my friend Melissa had messaged? Apprehension spiked at the thought of the outside world beyond the walls of my house. This was my home, but Kade had twisted it into little more than my prison. Now, I only sought to be free from it.

His gaze seared me as he grabbed my device. Rising from his seat, he wandered around my body and pressed the screen against my index finger. I sighed, knowing that one deed would unlock the phone and grant him access to everything he wanted.

"It doesn't sound as if your boss is too happy." Kade chuckled as he settled back on his stool. "He's not very empathetic, is he?"

Oh God. The ball of anxiety in my belly knotted until it was painful. What had Rex said, and how the hell was I going to talk my way out of this?

"What did he say, Master?" I was almost too afraid to ask.

"He seems to be inferring you only wanted today off for a long weekend." Kade turned the screen toward me, my eyes devouring Rex's reply.

Tiffany,

My knot of trepidation tightened. He only called me by my full name when he was pissed off.

Sorry to hear you're unwell, but it's hardly the best timing.

Rex was right. We had a mountain of cases, and I so wanted to lead on the new ones.

Rest up over the weekend, and I expect to see you on Monday.

Rex

Kade swiped the phone away as I digested Rex's words.

"Oh." I didn't know what else to say.

"Seems like he's in for disappointment." A conceited smile spread over Kade's attractive face. "You won't be in on Monday. In fact, I guarantee that your vomiting bug will spread well into at least next week."

"Master, please…" I shook my head. "I have cases I need to work on."

"All of which will surely survive your absence."

"But I don't want them to." I'd worked so damn hard on those cases, and every one before them—each had brought me to this point in my career. "I love what I do."

Kade's eyes darkened, warning of a storm to come.

"You'll learn to love new things," he assured me as his attention fell back to my phone. "Soon, you'll forget all about your career."

"But I—"

"That's enough," he snapped, rising to his feet and towering over me. "It seems like the privilege of a meal has gone straight to your head."

"I'm sorry," I panted, only too aware of how vulnerable I was if Kade's mood soured. I might not technically be bound to the stool, but my fetters gave me few options.

"Silence." He pressed his finger against my lips. "It looks like I've forgotten what my little girl needs." Turning to the counter, he grabbed a small apple and held it aloft.

"You need more than orgasms and omelets." His brow rose as he wandered back. "More than even punishment." Standing before me, he waved the fruit before my eyes. "You need constant guidance."

My gaze followed the apple as though I was hypnotized.

"Don't you, Tiffany?"

What the fuck did that mean?

"Y-Yes, Master."

"Yes, you do." He looked pleased with my answer. "When you don't receive the right guidance, you veer onto the wrong path, don't you?" Once more, his eyebrow arched as if it sought to taunt me.

"Y-Yes?"

"Yes," he confirmed. "That's on me, little girl. I should

know better than to let you wander, but don't worry, I'll learn. In fact, we'll learn together."

My belly churned at his menacing tone, though his intentions were still unclear.

"Good." His hand moved toward me, and my eyes flickered closed as it caressed my heating flesh. "Now, open."

My heart pounded faster at the command. *Open? Open what?* My legs were already forced apart, and—

"Open your mouth, little girl."

Lifting my chin, I locked gazes with him as his whole sordid plan fell into place.

"Master, please…"

"Don't make it harder on yourself." His tone was hard. "O-pen."

Pulling in a shaky breath, I stretched my lips wide, watching in horror as he moved the apple toward me and shoved it between my parted lips.

"Bite into this, and make sure you get a good grip—it won't be coming out for some time." The nefarious light in his gaze glimmered, sending panic pinballing in my mind.

He couldn't be serious, could he? He couldn't mean to gag me with my own bloody fruit? Even as I panted around the apple, I didn't know why I'd asked. Just look at everything Kade had the audacity to do. This was only the latest in a long list of daring moves—of course, he had the impudence!

"Bite."

Jolting at the deep resonance of his voice, I bit down before he had to repeat the order and sucked in the sweet taste of apple. My jaw ached as it strained to accommodate the fruit. The apple might not have seemed large in his enormous hand, but it sure felt that way forced into my mouth. Breathing around it, a line of juice made a denigrating track down my chin. Kade grinned as he stepped back to regard me.

"Good." He nodded at my apple-plugged mouth. "Now, my little girl will remember she doesn't speak unless she's spoken to."

CHAPTER 6: KADE

The emotions that flashed in her gaze were more gorgeous than I'd ever seen, a potent and giddy mix of fear, indignation, and arousal. Staring into her eyes, I could almost lose myself in their grandeur, but I didn't. This lesson was for Tiffany, not me.

Turning to the kitchen, I strode around, collecting what I required. Again, my prior knowledge of the place made the pursuit easy, and it didn't take long for me to return to the whimpering beauty.

"How are you doing, beautiful?" I placed the items on the marble island for her to see. "Enjoying your apple?" A desperate mewl escaped her throat, swelling my erection. "If you drop that fruit before I tell you to, there will be consequences." I inched closer, tipping her chin to meet my eyes. "Want to know what?" Her widening eyes suggested the answer was no, but I was reveling in her degradation far too much to stop.

"If that apple falls and hits the floor, we'll be using your phone to go live on Facebook." I chuckled as I motioned to the island. "A good old-fashioned spanking should do the trick, and I have the perfect utensil to help."

Her gaze flitted to the island, acknowledging the wooden spoon I'd selected. I wasn't sure Tiffany had ever been spanked by something as unrelenting as the spoon, but we would see how she dealt with its brutal rhythm.

"Understand?" I imagined pulling up a chair from the dining room and dragging her sorry ass over my lap for a hard spanking. The spoon would leave wonderful marks on her pert cheeks.

"Es, Aster," she mumbled around the fruit, the humiliating response doing little to quell my heating fervor.

"Good." I gestured to the spoon. "So, now you know what that's for." My lips stretched into a smile as I considered the clothespins beside the wooden spoon. "What about these, little girl?" Swiping them from the counter, I squeezed them open as I met her terrified eyes. "We both know you love these."

A defeated groan emerged from her throat, and even if she could have, I hoped Tiffany realized there was no point in denial. I had seen her search history and knew what turned her on, so there was little doubt she enjoyed the idea of attaching the pins to her exposed nipples. Reaching for her right tit, I lengthened the bud as she squirmed.

"These make a great alternative to clamps," I explained, allowing the wooden arms to pinch around her teat.

She moaned at the addition, her hips rocking as her eyes fluttered closed.

"Exactly," I enthused, switching to the other beading nipple.

A moment later, both were decorated with the clothespins, and Tiffany's reactions conveyed just how much she appreciated the steady pressure on her tits. Breasts like hers were made to be clamped and pegged. Readjusting my excitement, I reached for the spoon.

"Lovely." Wandering to her side, I flicked the clothespins nearest to me. "Now, open your knees."

Her gaze fixed on me as she slowly edged her knees apart. Leaning on the nearest one, I held it in place as I positioned the wooden spoon between her legs.

"This is how good girls behave—mouth silent, legs open, and tits completely at my disposal." I patted the head of the spoon gently at her sex, relishing the anguished cry that came from her apple-filled mouth. "Nonsense," I warned playfully. "I'm not hurting you, only reminding your clit who's in charge, just like I've reminded your mouth, tits, and ass." I grinned, recalling her backside still was still wonderfully full.

"Aster," she whined, her legs reflexively closing as the pace of the spoon intensified.

"Open," I growled, glowering until she complied. I sensed the level of effort it took for Tiffany to compel her knees back into position. "Now, keep them there." Adding a little more force, I angled the head, alternating strikes between her swollen clit and pussy lips. Each swat landed with a gratifying thwack, the noises increasingly wet as I picked up the pace.

"O od." Her head fell back, her shoulders tense with the effort of staying in place as her legs fought the desire to close.

"Yes," I praised, ensuring every third swat was much harder than the other two. The pain danced in her eyes as her gaze found mine, but her hips rocked toward the aggressor, seeking more of the spoon's sting and solace. "Very good, little girl."

Reaching into my pocket for my phone, I paused the

spanking and hit record before positioning the device on the island's counter.

"Aster?" Her brows knitted as her gaze darted between my face and the phone.

"Hush." Standing at her side, I fisted her hair, jerking her head back as the spoon resumed at her clit. She moaned at the competing sensations, her body coming to life right before my eyes. There was no need to command her knees to part now, no need to insist on their separation. Tiffany forced them apart, each smack jolting the clothespins as she arched between my hands, dancing to the beat of the wooden spoon.

"You. Will. Learn. Your. Place." I punctuated each word with a strike to her sex, smacking her labia before switching to her needy clit. "Gagged. Clamped. Plugged. And. Bound."

My cock strained to be free as I edged her closer to paradise. Turning toward my phone, I watched the act play out on the screen, the mirrored gesture ratcheting up my arousal.

"No. Speaking. Unless. I. Say." I struck her clit harder, enjoying her guttural cry. "No. Moving. Unless. You're Told."

Tiffany was suspended in my web as surely as a fly trapped by a spider.

"Eeese," she begged as the spanking continued, though I couldn't be sure if she was asking for the ordeal to stop or never end.

"Yes, little girl." I struck her one final time, lifting the spoon to the light as I fisted her hair harder. "You will learn."

CHAPTER 7: TIFFANY

I t was as if I was watching my life play out on screen, like all those filthy videos I'd watched over the years, except *I* was the heroine caught up in the deceptively hot plotline. More than aware of the sensations, I sensed the tug of the bondage and each vicious strike of the infernal wooden spoon, yet it was as though it wasn't happening to me.

"Eeese." The noise leaked from my throat, a response to the pain but also the burgeoning pleasure. However disturbing it was to admit, I was horny because of Kade's treatment. I loathed the sadist inflicting torment on my sensitive nub, yet I simultaneously adored him. I knew if he was to reach between my legs, he would discover just how much.

"Yes, little girl." He struck me again, lifting the spoon past my face as he jerked my head back harder. Electricity fired in my scalp as I struggled to alleviate the pressure. "You will learn."

A visceral silence bloomed between us, only the sound of my gasps filling the space as he held me there.

"My, my, my…"

I tensed at his cocky tone.

"Look how wet you are."

Squeezing my eyes closed, I gripped the fruit in my mouth. If he knew I was so aroused, why was he still tormenting me? Why wasn't he putting us both out of our misery?

"You are so perfect, little girl."

My eyes flew open at the noise of the spoon hitting the kitchen tiles, and my head turned against his chest.

"Up you get." He pushed me gently to my feet, dragging the stool away and standing flush against me. "So fucking perfect."

One of his hands slid down to my parted thighs while the other tugged at my pegged nipple. I cried out at the sudden hurt, though if truth be told, the pain only fueled my fire.

"I don't know how I lasted so long without you," Kade growled into the side of my neck as his fingers slipped between my wet lips.

I moaned as they teased, withdrawing and circling my frantic clit.

"Give me this." His free hand rose to my mouth, tapping the apple. "Now."

I spat the fruit out, stretching my jaw as he cast it aside.

"Has my little girl learned her lesson?"

My lesson? My brow creased. I was so turned on, I couldn't even remember what all of this had been about.

"Y-Yes, Master." I groaned as he cupped my sex, sliding one digit into my eager pussy. His intrusion was so good, I arched my back, silently begging him for more.

"Yes?" He sounded understandably skeptical. "You're sure?"

What the hell was he talking about? The man breaks into

my house, fetters, and dominates me, and now, what was this —a test? The pounding in my head was almost as insistent as my throbbing clitoris.

"Master!" I couldn't take much more of his teasing— either let me come or leave me the hell alone.

"Tell me what you learned." His dark chuckle circled as his finger coaxed another mewl from my lips. "Tell me, and you can have your pleasure."

"Fuck." I couldn't resist the word, the hedonism he created too much to tolerate.

"Tiff-any."

I clenched around his digit, aware of the menace in his tone.

"I'm sorry," I inhaled. "I learned not to speak unless you want me to." In the end, the words rattled from me as if Kade had conditioned them into me for years. My brows knitted as I contemplated that reality—he'd only had me for a few hours and had already taken me over on some subliminal level. What would happen if he took complete control? I might never get back the version of Tiffany I'd worked so hard to cultivate. I would never be the same.

"That's good." His hot breath tickled my ear lobe as a second finger joined his first. "You were paying attention. Good girl."

I had been, although I had no recollection of the learning.

"What do you get in return?"

Christ, he was playing with me again, wanting me to protract my humiliation, and the worst of it was, we both knew I would. We both knew I would not only say the words but relish every moment.

"The pleasure, Master." I was breathless. "Please, can I have the pleasure?"

"More pleasure?" He feigned disgust for the concept. "For such a greedy girl?"

"But I was good." My knees threatened to buckle as his fingers pumped in and out of me, his free arm snaking around me and pinning me against his body. "I did what you asked."

"Yes, you did."

I heard the smile on his face, and for the first time, I didn't despise it. Kade was one twisted son-of-a-bitch and had no right to do any of this, but I wasn't a fool—he was bloody gorgeous, and the limited time we'd spent together had persuaded me he was one hell of a masterful lover, perhaps even deserving of the title he so rapidly demanded. I didn't want to be caught in his web, but if I had to be—if there was no choice—then let him bring the hedonism. Let me drown in the tsunami of carnal delight Kade could deliver.

"Okay then." Kissing my nape, the palm of his hand grazed my clit, releasing fireworks in my mind. I was so turned on, I realized what he no doubt had already worked out—it wouldn't take much to push me over the precipice, right there in my fancy kitchen. "You'll have the pleasure, little girl, then you'll ensure your master is gratified."

"Yes!" I was pretty certain I'd have promised him the moon and stars if it meant reaching the orgasm I was chasing. Biting my lip, I rode his fingers, my hips driving my clit backward and forward over his hand as much as my trembling legs would permit. Oh God, I was so close. This was so wrong, yet my entire body was alive with sensation. The constant pressure of the clothespins on my nipples, the binds at my wrists, and the knowledge Kade was capturing most of this on the phone pointed in our direction—it was all too damn much.

Lips parted, I screamed as the wave of intensity broke, my body convulsing as he held me through the cycles of ecstasy.

"Master." The word was natural, my mouth perhaps understanding what my mind would never confess—any man who could make me feel this way was my master… carnally at least.

"I know," he snarled, already steering me toward the island. Holding me tight with one arm, he reached around my chest and released the clothespins. I winced as blood rushed to fill the tissue, but in a haze of euphoria, I couldn't call the sensation pain. It was more like freedom. Pulling in a deep breath, I was motionless as Kade cleared the counter-top, then repositioned the phone to face the new direction.

"I'm undoing these now." Tugging at my wrists, he released the ropes. I stretched my fingers as my arms fell heavily to my side. "Don't make me regret it."

"No." I could barely catch my breath, acting on autopilot as I heard his zipper lower from behind me.

"Hands on the counter." He was right there with me again, his stubble tickling my skin as he nuzzled my nape. "Now."

Lifting my hands, I looked at them as if they belonged to someone else. Once more, it was as though I wasn't really there—these things weren't really happening to me—as if I was witness to a salacious sexual marathon.

"Little girl." He swatted my ass with the growled warning, the sting snapping me from the hypnotic spell my climax had cast.

Placing my hands down, I stretched them across the cool marble.

"Better." His hands pulled my cheeks apart, massaging them roughly before he pushed against me, burying his hungry cock between my cheeks.

If there was any resistance within me, I waited for it to rear its head and make a case for why I should counter him. Why I could never accept his cock, should never consent, but I had already consented upstairs and didn't regret a single moment of that union. Kade was a messed-up fucker, but he was an exceptional lover. I had to get myself out of this intoxicating quandary, but not before I got what I wanted—what we both wanted.

"Master." I leaned over the counter, reveling in the cool temperature against my skin as I presented my ass to him. "Take what's yours."

Wait, what? Had I just said that?

Kade's laughter suggested he couldn't quite believe it either, but as he grabbed my hair and yanked my head back, his possession only ignited me.

"Not trying to take the lead, are we, little girl?"

"Oh, please." Grinding back against him, I no longer cared how I sounded, what I looked like, or that he'd was recording the whole bloody encounter for posterity. I just wanted him inside me, to fill me up and possess me. To make me feel like a woman.

"You want me, little girl?"

As if he had to fucking ask. I'd practically written him an invitation.

"Yes, Master."

There was no shame in saying so, no dishonor in asking for what I wanted. Kade knew me in a way no other lover had. He'd discovered my dark secrets and still craved me. In fact, it was those secrets that made me all the more alluring. I smiled, euphoric as I acknowledged my lack of embarrassment. A weight had lifted, as though his captivity had liberated me from the life I'd been forced to live before.

"Come on, then." Fisting my hair harder, he buried himself inside my sex.

My eyes fell closed at the sense of perfection, knowing this was what I'd missed. However satisfying my career was, however far up the corporate ladder I climbed, it would always come back to this—this insatiable need to be filled and used, a desire I had wrestled with for so long.

A guttural whimper escaped my lips as he moved, his fist holding me in place as he ground into me. All I could think as he took his fill was how right this was, how blissful. There were no thoughts of what came next, no concerns about tomorrow.

Kade was a dangerous virus who'd infected my life, but as he screwed me over my kitchen island, I didn't care. I deserved this pleasure, was worthy of fulfillment, and finally, I'd found a man who could deliver it.

"Fuck." He panted behind me, drawing me upright with his fist while his hips slammed his enormous cock into me. I complied like a good girl, reveling in his predatory dominance and the insanely good feeling of his dick. "Fuck, you feel incredible."

With my hands finally free, I reached behind his head, grasping his dark, luscious hair and arching for him as he claimed me.

"Yes," I agreed, my gaze flitting to the camera beside us. "Yes, Master. Fuck me."

CHAPTER 8: KADE

I t was an epiphany, a moment when every path I'd taken made sense. They had all been leading to this, this bliss, and even as the high ebbed, I knew it had been worth it. It had all been worth it. All the plotting and scheming, the sense of exclusion from my peers and read-justments, the terrible things I'd done—every one of them had led me to this cherished connection.

"Tiffany."

I couldn't believe how good she was, had never known chemistry like this. Hell, I'd even let her claw at my hair as we'd fucked, and to my surprise, I'd liked her urgency. She needed this—needed *me*. It was a revelation.

Stirring beneath me, her body was still strewn over the island where I'd pinned her as I emptied my cum inside her sex. Unpeeling from her hot flesh, I blew out a satisfied breath as I straightened. With her ass filled and her legs forced apart, Tiffany's cunt was glorious. There was no doubt—I was one lucky bastard to not only have found but claimed her.

Wrapping my arm around her middle, I hauled her

upright, resting her against me. Her head rolled back, a contented sigh leaving her lips. So, she'd enjoyed herself? It was one thing to take a woman by force—a trait I was well used to—but that wasn't how I wanted things to be with my little girl. I'd chosen her, not only for her looks and intelligence but for her proclivities, which were perfectly aligned with mine. Tiffany was the gorgeous little cumslut I'd spent my life searching for. She was the reason I could plan a life on the straight and narrow again, the light in a pitch-dark tale.

"You need a drink."

I shifted away, running a finger along her delicious skin. Skimming along her shoulder and down to the small of her back, I took a moment to appreciate every inch of her. It was strange, this need to nurture. Even though I acknowledged the reasoning—that she was my living, breathing orchid and needed care—it still perturbed. None of the others had been like this. They'd never roused such compassion. No doubt it was a sign of just how compatible we were.

"Yes, Master." Rousing, she twisted to meet my eyes. "Thank you."

Chuckling, I squeezed her cute little ass, suddenly reluctant to let her go. "I'll get us both a glass of water."

I moved away from the counter, already missing the heat of her flesh, and selected two clean glasses from the cupboard. Peering over my shoulder, I was relieved to see she was exactly where I had left her. Perhaps we had turned a corner in our growing dynamic. The knife attack had been a primal response to her abrupt incarceration. I didn't condone it but understood her reaction. This version of Tiffany seemed more resigned to her fate.

"Don't worry, Master." Her lips curled. "The knife block is way out of my reach."

My eyebrow arched at her wry tone. That was a brave comment for the naked girl I'd just fucked over the kitchen counter.

"I'm pleased to hear it."

"How is your neck?" Her voice was filled with hesitancy. "Would you like me to look at it, Master?"

"No, thank you." I smiled as I ran the cold tap, filling the glasses. "I think you've done enough for one day." Turning, I walked back to the island and placed one glass down in front of her. "Drink."

She met my eyes as she reached for the glass. An uneasy equilibrium seemed to have been established between us—she accepted my perverse games in return for untold pleasure. I would continue to push her boundaries, but our relationship was new and fragile like a ticking bomb. Any sudden moves could prove to be lethal.

I watched as she drained the glass, mirroring her actions until mine was empty.

"What now, Master?" She was trying to keep a respectful tone to show she had actually learned something from the last delicious lesson.

"Now, we rest." For so long, I'd sought a world where I could relax with my little cumslut, it almost didn't feel real. I smiled, realizing I'd finally manifested the woman of my dreams, and all it had taken was time, patience, and dedication.

"Let's go to the lounge," I decided out loud. "I'll open a bottle of red, and if you're a good footrest, you can enjoy some from Tabby's bowl."

Lips parted, face flushing, she absorbed my words. "I..." Her gaze fell as she struggled for the right words. "I didn't realize you'd met Tabby."

"Oh, yes." I grinned. "I met your pussy a while ago."

Tiffany bit her lip, unsure how to respond to my quip. "You'd make me drink from her bowl, Master?"

Fuck, the way she made that sound. "Of course." I leaned toward her. "It will be leashes and bowls for you whenever I say so."

"I see." Her pupils dilated as she shifted her weight from one bound foot to the other. "And the footrest?" Her question lingered in the air.

"You're the footrest," I reminded her. "And a bloody beautiful one. Now, which bottle would you recommend?" Placing my glass down, I rounded the island to plant a kiss on her shoulder.

"Something light at this time of the day," she murmured, "Maybe a merlot, Master?" Her brow furrowed, the weight of the obvious contradiction pressing down on her.

How could I want to objectify her one moment, then ask her opinion on vintage the next? I stifled my laughter at her puzzlement, the answer as perplexing to me as it probably was to her. I could shift so easily between gears because I—like Tiffany—understood the nature of the beasts lurking within us. Mine needed to be placated by humbling another, while hers craved the predator. Naturally, she had no idea just how dangerous that animal was, but with her, I was resolved to never cause lasting damage.

"I'll choose one." Cocooning her, I breathed in her sweet scent, promising myself that however tempting it was to confine her in some twisted way, I would reward us both with a night in her bed. I wanted to feel her soft skin and relish the heat of her body. "Will you be a good girl?"

She twisted back to meet my eyes. "Yes, Master."

"No playing with knives?" I glowered into her blue gaze. "In fact, no leaving this spot at all."

"I promise." She sounded so solemn as she made the vow as if an invisible jury was judging her performance.

"Good." Kissing the back of her neck, my cock stirred again. It didn't seem to matter how much I indulged my passion, when Tiffany was around, I could never get enough. "Place your palms on the counter." Arousal surged as I watched her obey. "I want those hands in the same spot when I get back," I told her. "Don't make me regret trusting you."

"I won't, Master." She licked her lips, her gaze flitting from my mouth to my eyes as if she was seriously contemplating stealing a kiss. "You'll only be in the hall and would hear if I move from this spot."

I smiled at her logic. Even in bare feet, I would be sensitive to her movement.

"I'll be back soon." Pushing my hair from my face, I stalked to the door, glancing back before I wandered into the grandiose hall.

"Don't forget what I told you." My voice was stern as it conveyed the warning. She might be as hot as hell and damn near impossible to resist, but I was serious. Tiffany wouldn't know what hit her if she moved from that spot.

"I won't, Master." Peering over her shoulder, her gaze ran over my body. "I won't forget."

CHAPTER 9: TIFFANY

My head spun as he disappeared into the hall. In my mind's eye, I saw his exact route—the walk I had made a thousand times before. The wine rack was between the aquarium and my mother's antique dresser, and the Merlots were stacked on the bottom level. I didn't know if Kade had already inspected my wine rack, but based on his apparent knowledge of just about everything, I had to assume he knew his way around and expected him to be efficient. By my rudimentary math, I had a couple minutes —maximum—before he was back by my side, bottle in hand, and ready to enact his next devilish scheme.

Heart racing, I considered my next move, my drying throat confirming what I didn't yet have the courage to admit. I was going to try to get myself out of this situation, fight to survive—what else could I do? Although the sexual rapture was heady and welcome, I couldn't go on like this, couldn't function in a world where compliance meant more than consent, but I had to be careful. The last time I tried, I'd been silly and reckless, injuring and upsetting Kade, which had only increased his determination to keep me. I had to be smarter, and whatever I was going to do, I had to do it fast.

I reached across the island for his phone as if it had been my plan all along, acting on autopilot, a default emergency version of myself I'd never needed to call on before. Kade seemed to have forgotten about the recording he'd left running, but I hadn't. Not used to being filmed all the time, my insides furled as I clasped the device, imagining all the ways he'd already captured humiliating scenes of me. The concept was new, exposing, and debilitating, but it offered me an olive branch. Fumbling with the controls, I clicked out of his camera and found his message box. My heart thundered as I created a new message, my every fiber attuned to what he was doing in the hall. I couldn't hear much movement, which meant he was probably choosing a bottle, and I didn't have long.

Quickly, my fingers moved over the screen.

Please help.

I sent the missive to 999, the UK emergency response, as a well of nausea surged. What if no one responded? What if someone called back and alerted Kade to my apparent duplicity? What if they didn't believe me? A myriad of fear and loathing swirled in my head.

I've been kidnapped inside my home.

3645 Pennsylvania Avenue.

This is his phone, so don't contact me on it.

"Are you being a good girl in there?" His voice floated in from the hall.

Glancing back in a panic, I was relieved to find he hadn't returned to catch me red-handed… yet.

"Y-Yes, Master." Shit, I sounded as fraught as I felt. My gaze scanned the message to ensure it had been sent.

With no time left, I skipped out of his messages, flicked

back into the camera, and restarted the recording. Leaning over the counter, I tried to position the phone in the same place he'd left it, dread escalating as I pressed my palms back onto the cold surface. Inhaling deeply, I fought to catch my breath and assuage my frayed nerves, afraid I would give myself away with my anxious performance.

Crippled with trepidation, the queries continued. Would he notice that I'd moved? Were my hands in a different place, and what about the phone—maybe it wasn't in the same position? Paranoia taunted me as I watched my pale face on the screen, my pulse racing so fast, I was almost lightheaded.

"How are you doing, little girl?"

I tensed, the volume of his voice telling me he was definitely in the doorway this time. Steadying myself, I turned to find him staring at me, gray eyes sparkling as he stood, bottle in hand. Pants undone at his hips, Kade was all rippling abs and enigmatic smile as he closed the distance between us.

"Good, Master." My eyes fluttered closed as he grabbed my ass, my rational mind fighting to stay in control. I couldn't give in to the combined visceral lust we created—not again. I had to stay alert and hope help would come.

"You certainly are." He chuckled, swatting my backside before placing his chosen bottle on the island between my palms. "South African red. What do you think?"

Was he seriously asking for my opinion? Earlier, he shoved an apple in my mouth and spanked me with my own kitchen utensil for so much as speaking out of line! My gaze darted around the place, wondering what had happened to the fruit. Kade's rationale made little sense. I couldn't keep up with the woman he wanted me to be.

"It's one of my favorites." Obviously, or I wouldn't have bought it.

"Excellent."

His hands ran over my body, grazing my goosing skin. I hated how he helped himself, how he thought he had the right, yet who was I kidding? I loved it. I'd never been more aroused than in the last few hours, but I had to be sensible. Carnality wasn't more important than my career, my liberty, and my life.

"I'll pour."

His large palms cupped my breasts, brushing over my nipples until I tried to jerk away. Trapped between his body and the counter, there was nowhere I could go. Nowhere to escape his roaming hands or his knowing tone.

"I can't wait to see you lapping from the cat's bowl."

Oh God, he was really going to make me do that? Panicking, my gaze slid to his phone, torn between the disgust that he was still recording and the desire to see if there'd been any reply.

You asked them not to reply. If they reply and Kade sees the message, you're fucked.

Unease snaked in the pit of my stomach as I imagined his response to what I knew he'd perceive as betrayal. Christ, he'd find a way of eluding the authorities, then think of a dastardly and disturbing way to punish me. I'd never be able to look at myself in the mirror again.

"How long have you been fantasizing about that?"

Just like that, he was in my kitchen dresser in search of a wine glass. My brow creased as I watched him choose one, sickened by how easily he knew his way around. He hadn't lied. He really had been there hiding, day after day, night after night. My head pounded with the sense of appalling violation.

"Little girl?" Kade's tone was stern as he spun back to glare at me.

"I-I…" Stammering, I tried to think of an answer. "I don't

know. For as long as I can remember." My toes curled into the cold tiles at the admission. Even after everything the man knew about me, it was excruciating to have to confess such private things—things no other living soul knew.

"I thought so." His lips curled as he reached back to select one of my favorite glasses. "It's good to be the man who finally brings this to life for you."

What the fuck was I supposed to say to that? Did he expect gratitude? His smirk suggested that yes, he did, but Kade was forgetting something important. I might easily get lost in the rhapsody of his dominance, but I'd never wanted this, never asked for the honor.

"What do you say?" His gaze bored into my face as he placed the glass down on the counter and lifted the bottle.

"Thank you, Master."

Heat burned my cheeks as I was forced to offer the humiliating reply. *That's the point.* I swallowed as the realization ricocheted around my head. *He wants to humiliate you, and he knows you like it.* Shit, I had to get away from him. I couldn't survive like this, couldn't reconcile my own base desires, let alone fulfill his.

"You're welcome." He eased off the screw top, breathing in the scent of the expensive red. "That's what I'm here for… to guide and demean you."

I clenched around the plug still shoved in my ass. I'd never worn it for so long before and was absurdly grateful to have chosen the smaller variety.

"I have to say I'm impressed." His eyes sparkled as he reached for my chest and tweaked my right nipple. "You haven't moved an inch since I went for the wine."

"You told me not to, Master." Tension careened through my body as he poured himself a glass.

"Good for you, little girl. Your master will reward you

once you've played the perfect footrest." His hand shifted to my other nipple, lengthening the bud until I groaned. "I know you like that." He grinned. "We'll get these beauties pegged again soon."

"Master…" I wanted to ask him what he was thinking, how he thought he could get away with treating me this way, but the words wouldn't come. After my audacity of contacting the police, the last thing I wanted to do was rock the boat and upset him. He'd made it clear that even speaking without permission was enough to land me in trouble.

"Hmmm?" His eyebrow cocked as if he couldn't believe it, either.

"I hope you enjoy the wine."

"Thank you, little girl." His face relaxed into a smile as he lifted the glass to his nose. "It smells divine, but I don't intend to leave you out. Drop to the tile and crawl to Tabby's cupboard."

"You want me to crawl, Master?" The butterflies in my belly, already overwrought with the experience, all flapped their wings at the same time.

"Absolutely." He gestured to the cupboard. "Pets crawl, don't they?"

My cheeks burned brighter at the horrifying rapture of what he described.

"You'll spend the next hour or so in a wonderful new combination of both pet and furniture." He laughed, sipping his wine. "Go on."

Not knowing what else to do, I fell to my knees and crawled the short distance to where I kept Tabby's essentials. I hadn't seen her since this ordeal started but could imagine her disdainful expression if she saw me performing for Kade. Cats had no master—neither coercion nor desire could force felines to comply. Tabby would never understand.

"I'd forgotten about the butt plug." Kade's laugh deepened as I crawled past him. "It looks beautiful shoved between those cheeks."

Oh God. When he talked that way, I didn't know what I was supposed to say, so I said nothing.

"Open the door, little girl."

Heart in my mouth, I rose to my knees and pulled the closet door open, revealing Tabby's food and toys. I couldn't shake the competing emotions wracking my senses. Fear about Kade's intentions coupled with concerns about the authorities receiving my plea fought my burgeoning arousal. Every time I lowered myself like this, passion pooled at the apex of my thighs, and I knew deep down, I ached for more.

"Do you see the spare kitty bowl at the back of the cupboard?"

"Yes, Master." My brow furrowed as my eyes fell upon the bowl. How had that got there? I hadn't purchased anything new for Tabby.

"Reach for it."

With one trembling hand, I grasped the china bowl, examining it as I pulled it out.

"Pass it to me."

I twisted on my knees, the motion awkward with my ankles still forced apart. By the time I turned, Kade was looming beside me, wineglass in one hand while the other palm was outstretched, waiting for my obedience. Lowering my gaze, I handed him the bowl.

"Wondering where the bowl came from?" He snickered as he placed it on the counter and poured the wine.

"Yes, Master." Of course, I wasn't. It was more than clear where the damn thing had come from. Just like the orchid, he must have bought it. The bowl was another example of how Kade had infested my life, and I hadn't even noticed.

"Consider it a present from me." Sipping at his wine, he smirked as he placed the glass down. "Look, I even personalized it for you." Picking up the china bowl, he lifted it toward me.

My pulse raced as my eyes took in the black letters printed on the edge.

Little Girl.

Fuck. You didn't get off-the-shelf cat bowls with those words printed on them. Kade had personalized it for me. Disquiet bloomed in my chest, a thousand silent warnings about the man who had the time and patience to play wicked games, but it was too late for all of them. Kade was there, in charge, and unless someone had seen my message and was prepared to help, he was—and would remain—my master.

"Now, it's time for you to use it." He placed the bowl on the floor in front of me, glee radiating from him in waves. "Come on, don't be shy." Pointing to the floor, he edged closer. "Try the wine."

My gaze flitted to his, my breath ragged. I'd daydreamed about being made to drink this way for so long, but the idea of actually having to do it—demean myself for his entertainment—was overwhelming.

"Why am I waiting, little girl?"

As ever, it was his steely snarl that made me move, my palms pressing into the white tiles as I inched toward the bowl.

"I'll help you." Kade barely suppressed his laughter as he collected my hair in his fist and pulled it away from my face. "That's better. Now I can see you blush as you lap. Wait, I need one more thing."

His hand released my hair, and he was gone in an instant. I swore my heart was ready to leap into my throat as I saw him grab his phone and flash the thing in front of me.

"I don't want to miss this, do I?"

Kade's insidious laughter echoed as he once again fisted my hair. Pushing the screen toward my burning cheeks, he lined up the shot he wanted as my panic blossomed. I had no way of knowing if the police had replied on Kade's phone and no way of controlling if he saw that hypothetical message. In fact, as his hand pushed me toward my fate, I couldn't even control my hammering heart.

Whatever happened, my plight was in his hands.

CHAPTER 10: KADE

"Face down." My cock throbbed as I pushed her toward the bowl. "Get your tongue into it."

She resisted at first, her body straining to stay upright, though I didn't know why. Tiffany and I both knew she was reveling in this. I'd seen the scenes she watched, fingered the paperbacks, and knew what got my little girl soaking with need. Pet play was one of those things, and I saw no shame in it.

"Oh God," she whimpered, panting over the wine.

"Go ahead and lap." I was enjoying myself, zooming in on her distressed expression while her mouth hovered over the liquid. "Remember, this is a privilege. I could choose to keep you gagged."

Heaving in a breath, her tongue probed the surface of the wine, lapping at it. A shot of triumph erupted, soaring through my system as I watched her. She was doing it! Finally, after all these years of craving and fantasy, I'd inspired her into action, and naturally, she looked incredible as she yielded. She pressed her palms into the tiles, lowering herself closer until my hand was no longer holding her in place, only keeping most of her beautiful dark mane from falling into her drink.

"How is it, little girl?" My voice was husky, conveying my need.

Her tongue hesitated as her gaze darted to me. Hot embarrassed cheeks flashed toward the camera, her mouth equally crimson from the mess she'd made with the wine, but it was her eyes that told the story. Undiluted disbelief gleamed in them as though she couldn't fathom what she'd become. Tiffany had never looked hotter.

"I want all that wine lapped up."

I panned the camera away, releasing her hair to get a great shot of her prone and plugged ass before scanning back to her dangling tits. She was so fucking delicious, as if she'd been made to serve me this way. The thought cemented, reminding me with surety that she had. Tiffany had been waiting for me her whole life—she just hadn't known it until I seized her in her sleep.

Grabbing the breast nearest to me, I massaged her mound roughly, pinching her nipple before reaching behind and slapping her backside. Her moan echoed in the kitchen.

"Why aren't you lapping?" I demanded, knowing full well why. I was distracting her with questions, pain, and stimulation, but Tiffany would need to get used to those challenges. Now that I had a pliant and naked little pet around the place, I'd indulge myself whenever the urge called—and it called a lot.

"Sorry, Master," she mumbled, her face already deep in the bowl again.

Stroking the outline of my cock through my pants, I was heady at the look of her. Christ, at this rate, I was going to shoot my load before she finished her bowl. I had to find a way to protract my pleasure. Switching off my phone without so much as looking at the screen, I slid the device into my back pocket and climbed between her splayed legs. Grazing one finger over her ass cheek, I smiled at the pink imprint my palm had left. Perhaps I would invest in one of those paddles with the word *pet* cut into the leather? I could emblazon the label on her like a brand, a semi-permanent reminder of what she was and who she belonged to.

Trailing my finger around the edge of the pretty plug still buried inside her backside, my digit slipped to her cunt. As expected, she was soaked with excitement.

"You like behaving like an animal, don't you?"

There was no need to ask; the evidence was there for both of us to enjoy, but where was the fun in silent observations? We both knew she needed me to highlight her perversity and deride her into rapture. While I didn't have any problem with her kinks, it was a role I was happy to play.

"Like being leashed, collared, and made to drink from pet bowls?"

Her head rose, the sound of panting filling the air.

"Don't you?" I slapped her ass, making her call out.

"Yes, Master."

My balls ached at the sweet sound of her anguish. It was tinged with just enough fervor to confirm she relished the treatment but left me in no doubt how torn she was about her predicament.

"Good." I stroked the same flesh I'd spanked. "Very good, little girl. From now on, you'll enjoy every drink from your bowl. I'll put it next to Tabby's. The only difference is she won't be leashed and can come and go as she pleases. You, on the other hand…" I chuckled, prying her delectable cheeks apart to reveal her glistening pussy. "You'll be chained up and compliant." Running my hands along her smooth skin, I allowed those words to sink in.

"On your knees now." I reached into my pocket as she moved, feeling for the two clothespins I'd removed earlier. Finding them, I waved the wooden pegs in front of her flustered face. I'd never seen Tiffany so hot and bothered, her gaze conveying her mortified arousal. "These are going back on."

"No, Master," she mumbled as I pinched the wooden handles. "Please."

"Yes," I reiterated, grasping her right tit and rolling her nipple between my thumb and finger. "I told you, I would decorate these whenever it suited me, and I like my furniture adorned when I use it."

Her gaze widened as the clothespin neared, but she accepted the hurt, catching her lower lip between her teeth, as one, then the other wooden teeth bit down on her sensitive teats.

"Better." I rose to my full height, grabbing the end of her long hair with one hand and my glass of wine with the other. "Come on."

Giving her little choice in the matter, I tugged her out of the kitchen into the sprawling lounge. Many the evening, I watched her relax in this room, watching some drivel on the television while glued to her devices, but that wouldn't be a problem for little Tiffany anymore. Now, her biggest concern was which hole I used or punished next. My cock swelled at our new delightful reality.

"I sit here." I purposely chose her usual chair, collapsing into it while she waited nervously on her hands and knees. Sipping my wine, I pointed to my feet. "You stay there."

She nodded miserably, the clothespins jutting out from her chest as I made myself comfortable. She was all too aware of what was coming next. I'd told her enough times, but there was something exquisite about watching as the piece fell into place in her mind. After so much pain and pleasure, I could finally relish every moment of her capitulation and see the minute nuisances that made her surrender special.

Resting my feet on her back, I reinforced the narrative. Tiffany was mine—mine to bind, gag, and degrade, and there wasn't a damn thing she could do about it. The very best thing, though, was deep down, I knew she didn't want to do anything. For all her desperate mewls and pitiful protests, she gave way every time, and her body revealed the real truth of her desire. I'd never known her wetter, never known any woman wetter than she was right now. Her passion betrayed her true feelings, even if she wasn't brave enough to admit them.

"This is the life, little girl." Swigging my wine, I considered flicking on the device she normally found so captivating. From this angle, with her head down and facing the far wall, Tiffany wouldn't be able to see what was on the screen. How demeaning would it be for her to be nothing more than furniture, not even be permitted to watch the equipment she'd found so bloody alluring?

"We need more of this." I stretched back into the chair, resting my neck as I pondered how to fill the rest of the day. My cock would need milking again soon, then perhaps I would continue her training on the contraption in the attic. The sooner she relaxed her gag reflex, the better. "More time to think."

"Y-Yes, Master."

I smiled at her shaky voice, imagining how she was feeling. After daydreaming about submission for so long, I was making all of Tiffany's hot fantasies come true. It would be like Christmas and Halloween—all rolled into one!

Vaguely aware of the noise of a car outside and the sound

of car doors closing, I glanced to the huge window behind me. In all the time I'd been hiding there, Tiffany rarely had visitors. My pulse quickened when I heard the voices—at least two people at the front of the house.

"Expecting guests, little girl?" My tone was wry, but my senses told me something wasn't right. Straightening, I eased my feet from her back and peered through her blinds.

My heart thundered as I took in the police car on the drive. Two uniformed officers patrolled the front garden, one diverting toward the front door.

"Shit." My brows knitted as I acknowledged I'd said the word out loud. "The police are here."

Shifting on her hands and knees, she glanced back at me with wide eyes at the precise moment there was a knock at the door.

"Did you call the fucking police?"

Rage rocketed through me. Either the authorities had taken to doing door-to-door house calls, or Tiffany had pulled the rug right out from under my feet.

Rising to her knees, she stared at me, her chest rising and falling, still pegged by the clothespins.

"Little girl." My voice was a soft growl. "Did you do this?"

How had she done this? I'd cut the landline, took her phone, and hadn't left her unattended with mine except…

Blowing out a breath, her whole sordid plan was revealed. She'd contacted the police while I chose the wine. The little bitch had used my own fucking phone to do it! The wound from her duplicity stung more profoundly than the blade.

"Hello!" The female officer knocked more loudly this time. "Is anyone there?"

"Help!" Tiffany was on her feet in a heartbeat, skirting around the coffee table and flinging herself toward the door. I'd never seen anyone move so fast with a spreader bar between their ankles. Time moved in slow motion as I lurched for her, grasping for her wrist, even as she threw her body weight against the door. She pounded her fists against the wood, screaming. "Help me! He's got me in here. Help!"

In that instant, everything unraveled. Tiffany didn't have the key, but she'd done enough damage, it hardly mattered. Even the most inept cop wouldn't leave after hearing an appeal like that.

"Hold on," the officer called. "You're safe. Stay there."

I backed away, nausea rising. This wasn't going to go the way I'd hoped, the way I'd planned. Tiffany had thrown a huge fucking hatchet at the plan. Running for the back door, I searched my pocket for the key, fumbling in my panic until my fingers clasped its familiar shape. Fastening my zipper, I pushed the key into the lock and turned. I'd let myself out the back way while the police were busy trying to gain access to the front. It was far from my ideal scenario, but it would see me away and safe—until I could find a route back to my traitorous little girl.

Thrusting the door open, I bolted outside—straight into the second uniformed officer.

"Now, where are you going?" He didn't look much older than twenty, but he was tall and broad enough to be a potential problem.

"Get the fuck away!" I hissed, shoving him as hard as I could before I ran for it.

Tearing across Tiffany's pristine back lawn, I rushed toward freedom.

CHAPTER 11: TIFFANY

"It's okay, Tiffany." The paramedic with the kind face smiled sympathetically as she wrapped the shiny blanket around my shoulders. Her lips kept moving, but I couldn't decipher her words. "You're going to be okay."

I stared at her as she checked my blood pressure for the hundredth time, wondering how many more of those feigned smiles I'd have to endure today. Time had been moving in odd pockets since the police had arrived. Initially, everything had slowed down to a crawl—each pounding of my fist on the door had seemed to take an hour, each breath painful and protracted. Once the house had flooded with uniforms, everything sped up to breakneck velocity. I could barely catch my breath, the urge to vomit looming as various authorities swarmed over my property. The sense of violation was vast and almost as perturbing as when Kade shoved his camera in my face.

"Have you eaten today?"

The paramedic tilted her head as though she'd been waiting for me to answer, but that wasn't right. I was sure she hadn't spoken, but then my head had become an echo chamber—a place absent of anything except numbness. Maybe she was speaking, and I just didn't understand.

Closing my eyes, I tried to recall the order of events since the police car had arrived, but it was impossible—the details were a blur I couldn't pin down. All I could see behind my eyelids was Kade—the curl of his lips and the sound of his deep laughter. I had to open my eyes again to make sure this wasn't all a dream, to ensure he wasn't towering beside me with a new demoralizing demand.

Even when the uniforms were finally in the house, it had taken a long time before I believed Kade had gone. They told me he had, told me he'd knocked their colleague to the ground and run for the hills, but I didn't believe them. I mean, I knew he *could* get away—he was easily strong and smart enough—but had he really? I still sensed him there, the scent of his body lingering like a specter, and even as I looked around, I expected to see his sinister grin lighting up the corner of the room. Like the Cheshire Cat in Alice's adventure, his smile haunted me still.

"She's in shock." The paramedic was chatting away, although I couldn't decide if she was talking to me. Glancing to my left, I realized she was deep in conversation with another police officer. "… Needs a complete once over at the hospital."

"Hospital," I repeated, though I didn't know how I felt about it.

"Yes," She patted my hand. "The doctor just needs to check you over. You've been through a lot."

"What about the house?" Sitting on my doorstep, I peered at the entranceway, and a low shiver ran down my spine. This place had been my dream home—the fruition of so many years of work, saving, and compromise. Now, it was polluted, each room a memory of Kade's invasion. I'd never be able to live in it again.

"You can come back as soon as you get the all-clear," she explained.

"No." I shook my head. "You don't understand. I can't be here."

The paramedic exchanged a glance with the police officer.

"Don't worry about that now," the cop said in the same soft tone the paramedic had employed. "It will take time."

"You don't understand." I was almost hyperventilating as I tried to get the words out. "He's all over this house. He has cameras everywhere." At least, that's what he'd told me, and I had no reason to believe he had only said so for effect. Kade had always been one step ahead—right from the beginning. Hell, he could even be recording this very conversation.

The cop's brow creased. "You're saying the man who did this to you has cameras in the house?"

"Yes." Why was it so difficult for her to grasp this? "He was living in my fucking attic without me even knowing." Tears welled as I finally said the words out loud. "He's everywhere."

"Okay." She patted me on the shoulder. "We'll lock the house up when we leave."

"He has the keys." The reality hit me in the face.

"What?"

"The keys to my house," I choked. "He stole my keys. If you lock it up, he can just come right back and wait for me all over again." My stomach knotted at the horrifying prospect.

"We'll leave officers on patrol," she reassured. "Until we can get the locks changed."

I nodded, knowing she was trying to be comforting but knew there was little anyone could do to offer solace. I could go through years of world-class therapy and scrub every inch of this place from the attic down, but the stain of what happened between Kade and me would always be present. He was a haunting I could never exorcise because he'd released the demons that lurked deep inside my soul. They would be with me wherever I went. There was no escaping Kade's legacy.

"Can you stand?"

The paramedic offered me her glove-clad hand, and wearily, I rose on shaky legs and glanced down at myself. They'd dressed me in awful medical scrubs, but I supposed they were better than the clothespins and butt plug I'd been wearing when the police first arrived.

"Come on." She guided me toward the waiting ambulance. "Let's get you checked out. The police will take care of everything else."

Walking the short distance to the ambulance, I paused as she lowered the ramp. Turning back to the house, my insides cramped with unease. Where was he? I half expected him to still be there, hiding inside. In those seconds before she gestured for me to climb on board, I could have sworn I saw his grin in the upstairs window.

CHAPTER 12: KADE

Unraveled. That's how I felt as I snatched the white shirt hanging from the garden line and tugged it around me. It was too small, but beggars couldn't be choosers. That's who I was now, at least in the short term —the beggar who needed to stay one step ahead of the law.

Three streets from Tiffany's house, I crept from the row of gardens that shielded me. Pulling the shirt closed, I struggled with the buttons.

How had it come to this? I'd had everything I wanted in the palm of my hand, yet somehow, I'd allowed it to slip away.

"You got sloppy," I muttered, stalking to the front of the row of houses and slowing to a more leisurely pace. I might be rattled but couldn't let it show. The area would be swarming with police, and I couldn't look suspicious. "You got sloppy and paid the price."

My jaw clenched as I pawed over what had transpired. I had left my phone running when I left the room while she was unbound. *I* had done that. Shaking my head, I blew out a furious breath, glancing into the front gardens of the passing houses. How had I been so fucking stupid?

Reaching for my phone, I flicked to my camera and searched through my recent videos. Hot, provocative images flashed before my eyes, displays of my little girl on her knees humbling herself on command. My feet stopped on the path as I pulled in a steadying breath. Fuck, she had been so perfect, yet I'd let her slip away. Whatever the pain was constricting in my chest, I deserved it. I merited this misery because I'd blown it. I'd given Tiffany a chance, and predictably, she'd taken it. I must have been a fool to think there would be any other outcome.

Compliant she could be, but she was no one's idiot. If I hadn't been clear about what an intelligent and creative creature like her thought about when it awoke bound and exposed, I sure as hell knew now. She thought about freedom, about clawing back her independence. For that, I couldn't blame her. This was all on me.

Scrolling back through the video, I relived the last hours in reverse, and my heart rate accelerated as the screen shifted position. Catching my breath, I found a quiet corner of the street and rested against a wall. I lowered the volume of the phone and replayed the relevant segment of the video.

"You're the footrest." I caught sight of my smirk as I teased her. "A bloody beautiful one. Now, which bottle would you recommend?" Placing my glass down, I rounded the marble counter to kiss her shoulder.

She looked delectable—nude and exposed—just the way I'd wanted her.

"Something light at this time of the day." Her gaze darted

behind her, and her breathing increased. "Maybe a merlot, Master?"

"I'll choose one." I pressed myself into her magnificent body.

My cock roused at the luck of the Kade on screen.

"Will you be a good girl?"

There was the question I'd been silly enough to ask aloud.

She turned back to meet my eyes. "Yes, Master." She didn't even flinch as she lied, the whole display captured by my device.

"No playing with knives?"

I had smiled as I warned her, a caution that had turned out to be irrelevant. She must have known what she planned to do once I'd left the room. It must have been her plan all along?

"In fact, no leaving this spot at all."

"I promise."

Once again, I was struck by the sincerity in her tone. Pausing the video, I glanced up, ensuring there were no unwelcome visitors. Seeing no one around, I hit play again.

"Good."

I saw myself nuzzling her and remembered how good she'd smelled when I breathed her in.

"Place your palms on the counter."

She obeyed with trembling hands.

"I want those hands in the same spot when I get back," I told her. "Don't make me regret trusting you."

I snorted at the irony of that comment. It suggested I knew all along leaving her was a bad idea, yet I still went, prioritizing wine and recklessness over common sense.

"I won't, Master." Her tone was breathy. "You'll only be in the hall and would hear if I move from this spot."

That settled the matter in my mind. Tiffany had definitely known what she was about to do. I could see in her expression that she had everything worked out.

"I'll be back soon."

I watched as I turned and walked to the door before pausing.

"Don't forget what I told you." My voice was firm.

Looking back, I wondered—had I known what was about to transpire? Was I setting a test for Tiffany that I knew she'd spectacularly fail?

"I won't, Master." She glanced back at me. "I won't forget."

The video played on after I had left the room. She was still for a moment, her breaths ragged as if she was contemplating her next move, then she reached for the device. I could scarcely catch my breath as she pulled it into her hands, bringing it to face level before the video abruptly halted.

Brows knitting, I skipped to the next saved recording, watching her startled expression as she tried to settle back in the same position I had left her in. Inhaling deeply, she fought to catch her breath before I came back into the room. The whole time I'd been out in the hall, selecting what I'd hoped would be an enjoyable red wine, she'd been in the kitchen, instigating my downfall.

Anger flared at the stark reality playing out. Naturally, I'd already concluded the truth, but seeing it play out in real-time was difficult to tolerate. I'd thought she'd been coming around to compliance, but she'd twisted the knife at her first opportunity. Tiffany had never given our dynamic a chance.

Her face was pale as she stared at the screen. No doubt she was worrying if the phone was in the right position, whether I would notice any difference, but she needn't have been concerned. I'd been so caught up in the growing thrall, I hadn't noticed a damn thing.

"How are you doing, little girl?"

Her body tensed as I appeared in the doorway behind her, the chosen bottle in my hand. Walking toward her, I grabbed her ass, never suspecting foul play because, for some ridiculous reason, I'd trusted her.

"Good, Master."

"You certainly are." I chuckled, swatting her backside before placing the chosen bottle on the island between her palms. "South African red. What do you think?"

I switched off the video, unable to stomach any more, accepting responsibility for my part. I should never have left her unsupervised, should never have trusted her, but still, the extent of her deception stung.

"Little girl." I swallowed back a well of emotion catching in my throat. "Little girl, what did you do?"

Sadness resounded in my tone as I exited my recordings and headed to my message box. Whatever she'd sent to the authorities could still be in my sent messages—she'd had little time to delete her missives. Taking a breath, I opened my last sent message. My heart hammered as I devoured the lines.

Please help.

I've been kidnapped inside my home.

3645 Pennsylvania Avenue.

This is his phone, so don't contact me on it.

The final fragments of my sanity dissolved as I reread the message, over and over. By the time I found the strength to keep walking, the words had been branded into my soul.

CHAPTER 13: TIFFANY

"**P**lease." I sighed, rubbing my temples. "We've been through all this already."

Hours had bled into days since the ambulance had taken me to the hospital, yet we were still going around in circles.

"I know, Miss Noble." Detective Constable Granger stopped scribbling and glanced up as if he couldn't believe my audacity. "But it's important we get the details right."

"You have the details." I met his eyes, weary from parroting the events over and over. As if it wasn't excruciating enough to admit the things Kade had made me do, the police also had access to the hours of recordings he'd set up around the house. It was increasingly difficult to look Granger, or any of them, in the face. "You have all the details."

I was the victim, but it wasn't hard to see the judgment flickering in their gazes.

If she liked that weird stuff, if that's what she'd pleasured herself to at home, how could Kade have truly coerced her?

It was as though I'd given consent by proxy.

"What else is there to say?"

"We know you're tired." Detective Sergeant Lucas smiled, trying to appease. "Are you getting any sleep?"

"Not much." Make that none. I'd moved into a hotel as soon as the hospital discharged me, only returning to the house to collect so-called essentials, with Melissa for support, but it didn't matter where I was. Apparently, there was no rest for women as wicked as me. "I can't get him out of my head." Crap, had I said that out loud?

"That's normal," DS Lucas assured me. "You're probably suffering from post-traumatic stress disorder. We can recommend a counselor to help you work through it."

Work through it? Was she joking? Kade had burst into my life and torn through the fabric of everything I held dear—all the accepted norms that ruled my life—and now, he was gone. No one knew where the hell he was.

"Where is he?" I glanced across the table at them. "Does anybody know?"

Granger pulled in a breath, then glanced at his superior. "There are no new leads for Mr. Walker."

"So, he just disappeared?" I threw my hands into the air. "Like magic?"

"He's on the run, Miss Noble." Lucas' tone was dry. "He'll slip up. Men like him always do."

"Do they?" I wasn't so sure. Weren't the newspapers filled with stories about men like Kade, men who eluded the authorities? I'd read those reports a thousand times, but now I was living in one of them. "So, he could be anywhere?" My gaze slid between them, ignoring the institutional cream walls, closing in with every passing moment.

"We can increase police protection if it'll give you peace of mind."

I sensed Lucas was running out of patience.

"It doesn't." I met her gaze, happy to confirm she wasn't the only one whose tolerance was running thin. I'd lost count of the number of hours I'd spent crammed into tiny interview rooms like this one since I'd left the hospital. I was shoved into suffocating rooms or forced back into isolation at the hotel and couldn't stand either. I wanted back my life, my privacy, and independence—a world where the entire world didn't think they knew who I was. I was done with their moral judgments. The inquisition could wait.

"I think we're done here." I rose from the seat, not waiting for their approval.

"But Miss Noble, we're only up to the morning after he revealed himself." Granger flicked back through the copious notes he'd made. "We need to go over everything else that happened between then and your first contact with us."

"Not today," I corrected him, striding for the door. "Today, I need air." I didn't know what crap they pumped into these police stations, but it never felt as if there was any oxygen.

"Miss Noble, I suggest you sit down."

My lips twitched at Lucas' firm tone. After spending several hours on tenterhooks with Kade's rumbling resonance, I was immune to the DS' attempts at sternness.

"I'm sorry." I turned, meeting her weary gaze. "Am I under arrest?"

"Well, no…" She flustered, smoothing down her skirt. "But we have assumed your cooperation, and—"

"You should never assume," I corrected. I'd learned that the hard way the night I'd woken up and realized my sanctuary had been thoroughly sullied by the menacing man with the piercing gray eyes. "If I'm not under arrest, I'm under no obligation to stay and answer the same questions again and again."

"That's true." Lucas' shoulders fell as she reached the same logical line of conclusion. "I'm sure you'd like to help us find Mr. Walker, though?"

"Yes." I swallowed at the sound of his name. *Mr. Walker.* It made him sound so formal and impressive, like a lofty professor, but that wasn't Kade. Kade was a machine made of muscle and ill-intent. He was dirtier, more visceral. He'd never be 'Mr. Walker' to me. *Master.* The title echoed in my head. *He's your master.* My hand balled into a fist at the unwelcome thought.

"You don't seem to be any closer to that eventuality." I glanced from Lucas to Granger, trying to control my swirling emotions. "You don't even have any sightings of him."

"Nothing we can confirm, no…" Granger's tone was hesitant, and not for the first time, I had the sense there was something he wasn't telling me, something they both were holding back. "But that doesn't mean we won't find him," he went on. "When we do, we'll need your full testimony."

"You'll have it," I reassured. "*When* you find him. Until then, we have been through this a dozen times, and you have the camera footage he left in my house." My toes curled in my shoes at the reminder of the mundane and mortifying they had access to—my life laid bare for strangers to paw over. It was the most soul-destroying feeling I'd ever known. "You know everything I can tell you."

"Okay, we understand." Lucas rose, wandering toward me, then paused as if she intended to offer me a hug but thought better of it. "Go back to the hotel and rest."

For fuck's sake. If I had a pound for the number of times someone had told me that since this all erupted, I'd be a millionaire.

"Thanks." I wanted to roll my eyes. Did she really think I

needed police permission to come and go? Christ, I was supposed to be the victim around here.

Turning, I walked to the door, pulled it open, and stalked into the military-gray corridor. If I'd hoped for a modicum of fresh air, the hall provided little respite, and I was practically running for the exit by the time it came into view. Flinging myself into the crappy parking lot, I doubled over as the damp air hit me.

Clouds had gathered since I'd gone into the station—an ominous metaphor for the way my life was going if ever I saw one—but I welcomed their intrusion. Cold water landing on my face broke through the barriers I'd erected, and though I had little desire to be drenched, I was relieved I could still feel *some*thing. Anything.

I forced myself to my feet and trudged back to the hotel, to another four walls that had effectively become my prison. Kade might be gone from my life, but his effects were everywhere, hemorrhaging in every direction. I hadn't been able to return Rex's calls or even look at my emails—work was mounting up around me like a volcano about to erupt. I couldn't even talk to Melissa about how I was feeling. She'd been understanding and called me every day, but I couldn't tell her the truth—how could I?

I didn't have the words for what was going on in my head —could never explain my confusion about Kade's treatment, never explain how, despite his disrespect, he'd touched something deep in my soul—when I didn't understand it myself.

Pacing past the reception desk, I stumbled into the elevator and hit the button for the seventh floor. By the time I arrived at my room, I couldn't decide if I was ready to scream, sleep, or burst into tears. Flinging down my purse, I allowed the heavy door to fall back as I closed the distance to the bed and collapsed across it. How long could I go on like this, living out of a suitcase because I was afraid to go home? My whole steady, consistent life had been flung into the air—thanks to Kade.

"Kade."

His name was a sigh on my lips. I'd so rarely been allowed to use it. Unlike Mr. Walker, Kade suited him perfectly. Ruthless, patient, and efficient—that was Kade. The kind of man who hid in your attic until he was ready to strike.

I inhaled at the wry realization. Rolling onto my left side, I saw it. The vase. On the vanity, opposite the huge antique mirror, was a bouquet in a large glass vase. The floral selection was obscured by the fancy paper wrapped around them. My brow furrowed, my heart beating faster as I stirred, rising to take a closer look. It wasn't until I was right on top of the vase I finally got a close look at the flowers, and what I saw almost took my breath away.

"My God!"

Stumbling back, my heart hammered as my calves hit the edge of the bed. I sunk to the mattress, but even as I sat, I knew I would get back up to find out how the bouquet had arrived in my room. Hand trembling, I peeled back the wrapping to reveal my favorite type of blooms—chrysanthemums.

Hyperventilating, I searched for a card—definitive proof they hadn't come from Kade—but frustratingly, there was nothing. Lurching for the telephone, I dialed the number for reception, actively working to calm my heart rate as I waited for someone to answer.

"Reception." The reply was as curt as ever.

"Hi, yes, I'm in room 725 and have arrived back to find a vase of flowers." I sensed the panic in my voice as I tried to explain. "Can you tell me who brought them, please? I didn't order them, and I don't see a note."

"Hold, please." As usual, the receptionist conveyed a staggering sense of concern. "I'll check for you."

Closing my eyes as she went to check, I consciously tried to slow my breathing. It was only a coincidence. It had to be. There was no way Kade could know I was here, no way he could discover my room number and smuggle flowers inside. If the man had any sense, he'd be long gone by now. He'd be—

"Miss Noble?"

My train of thought was obliterated as the receptionist interrupted me.

"Yes?"

"My colleague confirmed the flowers were delivered for you this morning."

My heart raced. "H-How did they get to my room?"

"They arrived with the vase and specific instructions," she went on. "We were asked to put the bouquet in the vase and leave it in your room."

"Oh." I glanced back at the vase, my mouth drying as I contemplated what she was telling me. "Thank you." I was still none the wiser, but nothing she'd told me had reassured the nefarious sense furling in my tummy. Something about the flowers was insidious.

"One other thing," the receptionist continued. "Apparently, there is a note."

"No," I countered. "I checked."

"Another of the instructions cited explicitly that we should leave it on your pillow."

Dread ballooned in my belly as my head turned in slow motion. There, sitting on the pillow I'd slept on since the whole ordeal had blown up in my face, was a card. Not listening to what the woman on the other end of the line was saying, my hands shook as I put the receiver down.

Time protracted as I moved toward the bed, each breath taunting as the pillow drew closer. Every fiber of my body was on high alert as I reached for the note, my fingertips skimming over the expensive card as I perched on the edge of the bed. There, in a handwritten calligraphic font, *Tiffany.*

"Oh God."

My voice was hoarse as I turned the piece of card in my hand. I played with the idea of throwing it away, chucking it out of the window, or burning it, but who was I kidding?. I had to know if it was him, had to know who was tormenting me. Reaching for the edge of the note, I pried it open and devoured the handwritten message inside.

Tiffany.

I saw these and thought of you.

My insides clenched as I read on.

You told me they're your favorites, and despite everything, you deserve them.

Know that when we're back together, I won't seek revenge.

Oh God, oh God. Terror surged, making it impossible to think.

I only want to continue where we left off.

Except this time, there'll be more chrysanthemums and fewer orchids.

Master

x

CHAPTER 14: KADE

Her face was priceless when she saw the flowers, sweeter than anything I'd seen since I left her side. Running my thumb over the screen, I smiled. My money had ensured the hotel staff had placed the vase with the hidden camera exactly where I'd asked, and now I got to enjoy the show.

Deep down, though, I yearned for more. I desired to see Tiffany's large, frightened eyes firsthand, to hold her as she trembled, to master her. I needed those things all the more now that I'd held them in the palm of my hands and let them slide away.

From my hotel room, I exhaled, recalling the final miserable moments inside Tiffany's house. It had all been so perfect—until she'd brought the whole thing crashing down around us like a house of cards. My brows knitted as I wrestled with the same rush of betrayal, the same sense of despair, and the primal need to be back with her. I missed Tiffany—the color of her hair and the tiny throaty gasps she took when she came. I missed everything about her.

The spiraling events after I'd made a break from her back

door were a haze. I vaguely remembered the cop and his shocked expression when I sent him smashing to the concrete. I might have been unprepared for the mad dash that ensued, but my reflexes were as honed as ever. Responding out of instinct, I'd floored the poor sod, leaving him dazed as I darted from the property.

That had been days ago. Hours without my little girl, time neither of us could take back. My heart ached at the gloomy reality, but the melancholy hadn't stopped me. The back alleys gave me time to take stock, and my phone had only expedited the process. Drawing on my vast funds, I was soon rested, clean, and fed. Hacking the police's poorly protected systems, I'd discovered where they had housed Tiffany. I checked myself into the same hotel the next day, using a pseudonym and taking its most expensive suite. Nobody, neither plain-clothed officer nor staff member, had so much as blinked as I took residence. It had been ridiculously easy.

From my suite, I monitored the comings and goings of room 725, knowing it housed what was mine. Tiffany only left to meet detectives handling her case who, I assumed, took her to the nearest station for questioning. I could have verified the point had I the will, but I knew how the British criminal justice system worked and had little inclination. They would take her and ask her the same repetitive queries, but my little girl knew nothing.

She didn't know where I'd come from. Hell, she didn't even know how long I'd been hiding in her attic. I watched with a heavy heart as the police dismantled the cameras I'd secreted around her home, but I didn't allow it to get me down. Better to spend the time she was absent working on how to seize her back, but more importantly, how to woo her. Tiffany had warmed to me over the hours I'd toyed with her, and despite her repeated offenses, I knew, deep down, she craved my time and attention.

Now that I had hotel staff on my payroll, she would soon have it again.

Grinning, I flicked back into my device. It had been easy to replace my old charger, just as it was easy to trace Tiffany. Money bought influence and power, and coupled with my knowledge of how to get away with murder, the authorities didn't stand a chance. Watching the camera, my smile widened at the scene that met my eyes. Thanks to the hand-delivered vase of Tiffany's favorite bloom, I was now privy to a new and exclusive perspective into her small hotel room.

Turning up the sound on my device, my gaze bored into the screen. The angle wasn't perfect, but I could see her sitting on the double bed, clutching what looked like the card I'd sent.

"Oh God." Her brow furrowed as she glanced at it again. "Oh God, he knows where I am!"

"That's right, little girl."

I wanted to march down there and drag her back to my suite for a damn good spanking, but even my exhilarated rush of joy at seeing her again wasn't enough to lull me into a false sense of security. James, the staff member who'd taken my money for the favor, had confirmed there were police routinely guarding room 725, and while none of them had been smart enough to notice me in the bars and foyer, they might just start paying attention if I walked up to her room and knocked on the door.

No, if I wanted Tiffany—and I was in no doubt she was mine—I'd have to be more intelligent.

Reaching into the top drawer of the bedside counter, my fingertips skimmed over the spare device I'd ordered. I had designated a special use for the unused second mobile.

Punching in Tiffany's mobile number, I smiled as I started a new message. I hadn't known her number before her run-in with the police, but their systems enabled me to help myself to her personal details.

Do you like your flowers, little girl?

Hitting send, my heart raced as I watched her respond to the incoming message. Sadly, not all of her gorgeous face was visible from the fixed vase camera, but her body language was, and I witnessed the moment she read my question.

"No!" A strangled mewl escaped her lips as her fingers clutched her phone so hard, they looked white on my small screen. "Please, no."

My cock stirred at her desperation, and as she rose from her bed, I wondered what she'd do next. Would she contact the ludicrous detectives who'd been hounding her since I fled her house? I doubted it. Tiffany had arrived at the hotel earlier than the prior day, suggesting their rounds of questions were unsatisfactory. I'm sure she was finding out the police were every bit as intrusive as I was, without the added impetus of rewarding pleasure to look forward to. My unspoken query was answered as she staggered toward the camera, leaning against the dresser as her fingers flew over her device. Moments later, my pulse quickened when my phone vibrated.

Kade, please don't do this.

My lips curled at her choice. I didn't like how she'd addressed me, but that she'd replied at all was immensely pleasing. Back at the house, Tiffany might have called for help, but evidently, she was still torn. I had created that blissful quandary. She wasn't sure if she still sought the so-called liberation she thought she wanted or if she should succumb to the baser needs she knew I could gratify.

What was that, little girl? I didn't think twice about

answering as I flicked back into the view of the camera in time to see her reeling back to the bed.

"No." Her hand rose to her mouth, and from the grainy image, I could just make out tears in her eyes. Her hands trembled as she grasped the phone, her chest rising and falling in the rapid way I enjoyed.

Triumph soared as I watched her unravel, the fear and malcontent she'd bottled up releasing as she stared at her device. Smirking, I returned to my message, following up with another.

You know how to refer to your master.

Her on-screen image inhaled, steeling herself as she responded.

What do you want, Master?

Arousal surged as she capitulated to my demand.

You, little girl.

There was no hesitation as I laid it on the line. I'd worked so damn hard to get to this point, waited so long to make her mine, I wouldn't let Tiffany's bout of nerves destroy everything I had created.

I don't like what you did, but I understand, and I'm ready to carry on where we left off.

Unable to see her face while I typed, I gripped the handset, imagining her expression as she read my lines. Would they please, scare, or excite her?

I can't.

My heart skipped a beat. I fumbled with the keyboard, considering how to answer, when another missive flew into my inbox.

I mean, I can't go back to how things were at the house, Master.
I need more than that.

Pulling in a deep breath, I paused. She needed more? My brows knitted at the disconcerting thought. I had meticulously planned Tiffany's treatment. I'd done my homework and learned everything that would rouse and liquefy her. What more could she possibly need than a man who was prepared to make her the center of his whole fucking universe?

Flicking back to the camera in her room, she was sitting on the bed, fidgeting with her phone. Clearly agitated, she refreshed the screen, apparently waiting for my reply. It was pleasing she wanted to exchange messages... great news she wanted to communicate at all. She could have contacted the useless detectives she'd been talking to, could have reported me, but she hadn't. Whatever alleged concerns Tiffany had, they weren't strong enough to control her. They hadn't stopped her from reaching back to the monster who'd captured her.

Master?

She glanced up at the vase as she sent the follow-up, staring straight into the camera. If I didn't know better, I'd have sworn she knew it was there.

I considered berating her for making demands. In normal events, she wouldn't have been in a position to negotiate, but Tiffany had changed the rules of my game when she'd reached out to the authorities. She'd turned the tables, granting herself power, and though I loathed to admit it, I recognized I would cede to her new sovereignty.

I'd lived without Tiffany and knew how that desolation felt. All those years prior to knowing her, the era of bloodlust when numerous pretty young things had fallen foul of my desires. I didn't want to return to that dark place, couldn't risk being that man again.

Releasing the breath I wasn't aware I'd been holding, I acknowledged what was obvious. I would relent if it meant getting her back. I would do the one thing I'd never done before—compromise.

What do you need, little girl?

I stared at her wide eyes, witnessing the moment she gasped. Tucking her hair behind her ears, one of her small hands rose to her mouth. Evidently, she was having trouble believing I'd asked. Slowly, her fingers replied, her gaze flitting periodically from her screen to the flowers hiding my camera.

Respect, Master.

Her request leapt out, slapping my face.

I love the thought of the things you do to me, and yes, my body enjoys those things, but I'm not your property. I deserve to be treated with respect.

I reread those lines three times before switching back to the camera, observing her gorgeous features. How had Tiffany bewitched me? Sure, she was as sexy as hell, but so were a thousand women before her. What was it about the captivating brunette that made her impossible to leave behind?

Skimming my finger over the screen, I remembered how soft her skin was. Christ, she was amazing to hold... to touch. I wanted that again, had to have her. Tiffany was different from all those others, exponentially more than desirable. She had more going for her, a brain as well as a beautiful body. She'd made a life for herself, one worthy of my inclusion but needed an injection of my mastery. Intellectually smart, but I couldn't always tell based on the way she lived her life. She worked too many hours, didn't eat well, and never got enough exercise. Tiffany was careening toward total wipeout, and I had been sent to save her—she just didn't know it yet.

Meet with me, and we'll talk about it.

It was time I took the reins again, but I had to do so gently.

Meet you? Are you mad, Master? How can I do that? I'm holed up in a hotel, and there are police everywhere.

I chuckled at her naivety.

It's simple enough, beautiful. Take your room key and go up to the tenth floor.

Flicking back to the camera, I caught sight of her astonished visage.

The tenth floor?

She nibbled her lower lip as she sent the missive.

That's right, little girl.

Christ, what I would have given to hold her at that exact moment, to have witnessed the wonder in her gaze firsthand, rather than on my minute screen.

You'll find me in the Royal Suite.

CHAPTER 15: TIFFANY

Whatever fragments of my sanity I'd clawed back over the last few days evaporated with his message.

You'll find me in the Royal Suite.

The Royal Suite? The Royal Suite in this fucking hotel? The butterflies that danced in my belly huddled, knotting into an amorphous ball of churning apprehension. Kade was in this hotel? Oh, fuck...

My heart raced as I tried to fathom what he was telling me. If Kade was there, what the hell did that mean? Had he been there all along? Had he seen me, been watching me again? Panic flared in my chest, capturing my anxiety and threatening to send the lurid combination to meet the back of the toilet seat.

"Oh God."

Closing my eyes, I tried to calm my breathing, but I felt as if I was breaking inside. How could any man affect me so profoundly, let alone one who'd done such heinous things? Kade had violated my home, my privacy, just about every right I'd taken for granted, and reveled in my suffering. He was a fucking fiend, so why wasn't I running for the officer stationed in the foyer or calling DS Lucas? Why had I replied to his unwelcome advances?

"Because they're not unwelcome." The answer was as obvious as the horror-stricken look on my face in the mirror behind the chrysanthemums when I opened my eyes. "You want this," I whispered, rising from the bed and wandering closer to my reflection. "It doesn't matter what you tell the police or anyone else. You know you wanted it." Heaving in a breath, I shook my head at the hapless woman in the glass. "You fucking wanted it. You were just scared of him—*by* him —that's all."

Fuck. Moving past the dresser, I rested my head against the mirror, steaming the glass with my breath. I had wanted Kade's treatment—even though I hadn't agreed to it and certainly hadn't given him permission to be in my house. My body had betrayed my true response to his schemes.

I'd spent my life suppressing my cravings, ignoring the dark desires raging inside me, and choosing to focus on work instead of passion. In all that time, had I been happy with my choices? My brow furrowed at the question, though I already knew the answer. No. I'd never experienced real lust before Kade, hadn't known how deep the yearning could be.

That first night he'd taken me to the attic, everything changed. As well as the fear that had coursed through me, there had been something else, something stirring that had shaken my soul—an awakening, awareness I'd finally collided with feelings I couldn't fight. Despite the distress, I didn't regret those emotions.

Managing a small smile, I relaxed into my new self-awareness. If nothing else, Kade had brought me a sense of who I was—a tsunami washing away all doubt on the subject.

The vibration of my phone in my hand brought me back to the then and there.

Tiffany.

I tensed at that one word, already sensing Kade's tone.

Why am I waiting, little girl?

Leaning against the glass, I pulled in a breath as I replied.

You're in the hotel, Master?

That's right. You had better be on your way to my suite right now.

Anxiety furled in my tummy, bubbling alongside my brimming excitement. Kade was here! There was no way that should be as intoxicating as it sounded in my head.

I'm coming, Master.

It was the most ludicrous decision of my whole life. Grabbing my keycard, I darted for the door and scurried down the hallway toward the stairwell. My heart pounded in my ears as I threw open the door and started up the steps. I shouldn't be doing this, shouldn't have even communicated with him, let alone indulging his whim or contemplating seeing him again, yet there I was, already on my way to his suite. Pausing at the entrance to the tenth floor, I gripped the railing as I pulled in a shaky breath. Was I eager to see him or sick with nerves? Could it be possible both were true?

My pulse leapt when my phone vibrated once more. My gaze devoured his message as I lurched onto the tenth-floor corridor.

Oh no, little girl. You don't get to come. Not until I say so...

My lips curled at his command, distracting me from my pursuit.

Why aren't you here yet?

Identifying a sign, I headed toward his suite, forcing myself to take deep, steadying breaths.

I'm close, Master.

God help me, I was actually enjoying myself as I wandered the hallway.

Just looking for your room.

I didn't know what was wrong with me, but I'd missed this. This odd taste in my mouth and the way my heart sped up. This bizarre and dangerous dynamic Kade and I had conjured. My life had reverted to monotone without it.

"I see you, little girl."

My feet paused at the sound of his voice, and glancing up, he was right there, looming in the only doorway ahead.

"Fuck." I hadn't meant to say the word aloud but was vaguely aware it leaked from my lips. Kade was even more than I recalled—taller, darker, and more impossibly good-looking. Coming up here had been a mistake. How could I ever walk away from a man who looked like him, knowing how he could electrify my life?

"That's very forward of you." His lips stretched into a handsome smile. "I thought you only came to talk?"

"I…" My voice trailed away, heat rising to my face as I struggled with what to say. This wasn't the most embarrassing situation I'd been in with Kade, wasn't even close. So, why was I so flustered? I'd come to discuss things with him, to take back the control I'd so fleetingly held when that blade had been in my hand, but even as I wrestled with the notion, I knew it was a lie. I'd never had control where Kade was concerned and didn't want it. I only wanted to be treated with dignity—as well as the degradation.

"Little girl?" He smirked, tilting his head as he beckoned me forward with one finger. "What's wrong? Cat got your tongue?"

"I didn't think I'd ever see you again," I admitted, closing the distance between us. It seemed significant that I was the one walking toward him, each small step my choice this time. "Master."

Saying it out loud again was the most perturbing of all. Glancing behind me quickly, I realized there was no one else there. No one to witness my denigration. No one to see me as I slipped into his lair.

"No." His expression was serious as I stood before him, his hands shoved into his pockets as if he needed the reminder I wasn't there to be touched. "I don't suppose you did."

Peering past his shoulder, my gaze wandered into the suite behind him.

"Do you want me to apologize?"

"For what?" Kade's brow rose.

"For contacting the authorities, Master." My concentration flitted back to him.

"Do you want to apologize?"

"I…" I hesitated, musing on my answer. Was I sorry? "I don't know. I was desperate. I couldn't take much more."

"I think you could have taken a lot more." His voice was even as one of his hands relented, rising to my chin, every fiber of my being paralyzed by its journey. Caressing the edge of my jaw, he nudged it compelling me to meet his silver eyes. "But I understand your comments about respect and needing more."

"You do?" My brows knitted, barely able to comprehend what I was hearing. Kade, the monster who'd lurked in the shadows for so long, was talking about acknowledging my worth. Well, that was a first.

"Yes." He suppressed a chuckle, stroking the underside of my chin. "I know I haven't focused much on those things."

"Or consent." My gaze burned into his, acknowledging

this might be the first and last chance I was able to say these things.

"No," he agreed. "Nor consent."

"That's what you want to talk to me about, Master?" My heart raced harder with every brush of his thumb.

"Yes." His face relaxed. "That and anything else you'd like to discuss, but you still haven't answered my question, little girl. Are you sorry for involving the police?"

I peered around again at the mention of the authorities. Lucas kept officers stationed in the hotel, and it was dangerous to even have this conversation, but the idea of moving inside his suite was overwhelming. My attention darted back through the door again, imagining what it was like inside. Did I want to go in and discover for myself?

"It's okay," he soothed. "It's only us."

"I just needed some time…" I forced myself to articulate the labyrinth of feeling he'd roused in me. "Time to think about you and what I wanted. I didn't know another way to make you stop, Master."

A glimmer of hurt flickered in his gray gaze, or maybe I only hoped it was hurt. Could a man like Kade feel the same emotions I did? Then, if I truly believed that, why was I with him again?

"I guess I didn't give you many options, huh?" His lips twitched.

"No, you were…" I paused, trying to think of the right words.

"Demanding?" he suggested wryly.

That was one way of putting it!

"Yes, Master." I relaxed a little as I was finally allowed to voice my opinion. "A bit too demanding."

"I enjoy demanding things from you." He leaned closer,

brushing his fingers across my cheek. "I'm not sure I can promise I'll change."

Staring into his mesmerizing gaze, I ignored the red flags waving in all directions and stumbled through the flashing signs. No rational part of my brain should have permitted me to come this far, let alone consider taking me inside his suite, but there it was—his open doorway suddenly the object of both my curiosity and desire.

"I didn't think you would change."

Then, what the hell are you doing there? If he's not changing, then you're only walking back into the web he's spun for you...

"Your messages inferred you wanted a change." His lips curled. "Needed more respect."

"Yes." Christ, I wasn't even making sense. "I can't continue the ways things were, but…" My throat dried as the enormity of what was coming next crashed over me.

"But what, little girl?" His hand rose to my hair, tugging my tresses from my face. "Tell me."

"There must be a way forward that can keep us both happy, Master." I could hardly get the words out. "A more respectful way to live out our fantasies."

"What an interesting idea." He flashed me a devastating smile, revealing a line of white teeth. "Would you like to come inside and talk it through?"

CHAPTER 16: KADE

Tiffany was so diminutive, standing beside me in the hall. Dressed in casual joggers and a t-shirt, she was every ounce as stunning as I recalled.

"What will you do to me inside, Master?" Her blue eyes flashed with her warring emotions.

So, she wanted assurances? That was understandable, but I couldn't resist the wave of amusement that rained over me. Poor little girl. She had no idea what would happen when I swept her inside... but then, neither did I.

I knew what I was capable of but wanted desperately not to cede to *that* man's appetite for destruction. If I wanted this budding desire between us to blossom, I had to play the next hand carefully. On more than one occasion, Tiffany had proven she was able and willing to counter me. My free hand rose to my neck, the scar she'd given me still healing. The woman had hurt me and forced me to flee. Evidently, she was pretty capable herself.

"I won't touch you until you ask me to." Releasing her, I shoved my hands down to my sides. "Whatever happens next, I want to know you want it."

My brow rose as I acknowledged, for the first time in my whole life, I actually meant it. From this point on, Tiffany's consent was critical. I'd spent so long taking what I wanted, it was astonishing to finally acknowledge it. Deep in my soul, I needed to make good on all the fucked-up things I'd done, and Tiffany was my one hope of redemption.

"Do you mean that, Master?" Her wild eyes demanded I say the words again.

"I do." Fuck, I already regretted my vow. The longing to reach for her, touch her, and guide her into the suite was almost overpowering. "If you come inside, I'll make you a drink and listen to what you have to say."

"What about the police?" Agitated, she shifted from one foot to the other as if she was the one on the run from the law.

"They don't know I'm here," I assured her. "And if we get out of the hallway, we can keep it that way."

"O-Okay." With a small smile, she side-stepped me as she turned toward the suite door. "I can't believe I'm doing this."

I knew what she meant, but watching her approach the threshold was the closest thing I'd felt to joy since the cops had knocked on her door. Waiting until she'd passed into the suite's entrance hall, I followed and closed the door behind me.

"Are you locking the door, Master?" She didn't glance back, but her voice was etched with trepidation.

"No, little girl." The urge to stroll behind her and nuzzle her heavenly neck gripped me, forcing my feet to stop. "It's not locked."

She peered back at me. "Thank you."

Our eyes met, and I noticed how hard she was working to diminish the panic spiraling in her eyes. Perhaps as hard as I was trying not to march over there and claim her sweet mouth.

"Please, go through to the lounge." I gestured to her left.

"There's a lounge?" Her gaze widened.

"Yes." I smiled. "A lounge, a dining room, a kitchen area, and two bedrooms. It's all rather indulgent, to be honest."

"This place must cost a fortune." Her gaze went to the ornate ceiling above us.

"Yes, it's…" I paused, enthralled by her flushed expression. "Not the most economical choice, but I know what I like, little girl." I grinned as her gaze landed back on me. "When I find something I want, I go right after it."

"I see that." Pulling her lower lip between her teeth, she nibbled.

"So, the lounge?" I tilted my head in its direction.

"Oh, yes." Fresh heat pooled in her cheeks. "Right."

Tiffany sashayed away, the allure of her hips compelling my feet to follow.

"What would you like to drink, little girl?"

She turned, awestruck as she took in the expensive décor.

"I would say red wine, but…" Her lips curled. "The last time I enjoyed it, someone drugged me."

Chuckling at her audacious response, my cock swelled at her furtive smile. Tiffany was adorable. Face down over my knee or engaging me in conversation, I couldn't get enough of her. Watching as she inched closer to where I stood, I acknowledged how much I wanted to share all those experiences with her. Tiffany wasn't a disposable pleasure. I'd been right all along. She was a keeper.

"Fair point," I replied with a smile. "You're welcome to check that I haven't tampered with any of the bottles."

"You know, I might just do that, Master." Breath ragged, she walked toward me. "Where do you keep them?"

"In the dining room." I signaled back the way we'd come. "Follow me." Spinning on my heel, I strode through the foyer into the luxurious dining area. There, on the rosewood table, were three bottles of red wine. "Care to choose one, little girl?"

She stepped forward, her gaze once more traveling around the place before she focused on the choices. "I like Italian wine." Grasping the Sicilian red, she examined the top to find it still corked and encased in its original wrapping. Her lips twitched as she turned to me.

"Happy?" My eyebrow arched as she presented the bottle to me.

"Yes, Master."

"Good selection." Reaching for the bottle, my hand brushed hers as she permitted me to take it. "Go back to the lounge. I'll open it for us and pour."

She loitered in the doorway for a moment, watching as I selected two glasses.

"Problem?" Glancing over my shoulder, I met her eyes.

"No, Master."

Fire burned in her brilliant blue gaze, flames that spoke of passion and unbridled need. Tiffany only had to say the word, and I would stoke those flames, but in the short term, I had given her all the leverage.

"Go then."

She disappeared from view as I unwrapped the top of the cork and eased it from the bottle. Allowing it to breathe, I grabbed the glasses before striding to the lounge. Curled up on one of the oversized couches, Tiffany looked even smaller against the enormous cushions. Setting the glasses down, I poured the wine, offering her one of the delicate stemmed glasses.

"Thank you, Master."

I made myself sit on the opposite sofa in case the temptation to reach for her became intolerable. "You're welcome. Now, where do we begin?"

"So much has happened." She blew out a breath as though she had been wondering the same.

I laughed gently at her grave analysis. "You make everything sound daunting and awful. I recall a little girl who reveled in a lot of pleasure."

Her eyes fluttered closed. "Yes, there was pleasure."

"Why don't we start there?" I suggested, lifting the glass to my nose and inhaling the wine's blackcurrant aroma. "Tell me what you liked about being my little girl." I didn't know why I phrased the question in the past tense. Tiffany was still my little girl and always would be.

"The sex was incredible." Her voice was little more than a squeak. "I've never known anything like it before."

"Mmmm." My lips stretched into a wide smile. " I remember."

"You know how to drive me wild with passion, Master." She shook her head as if she couldn't believe the things we'd done. "You know all the ways to turn me on."

"You were always so wet for me." I couldn't resist my smug tone or the way my cock sprung to life inside my pants.

"Yes." She breathed in a shaky breath as if she were confessing to her priest.

I chuckled at the analogy. In some ways, it was fitting, except if all went well, I would be more like a god to the flustering brunette.

"And I liked it when you cooked for me, Master." Her blush deepened. "No one had ever done that before."

"No one?" It was my turn to shake my head. "You must have had some terrible boyfriends, little girl."

"Yeah." She sighed. "They weren't great..." She hesitated. "And there's been no one for a long time."

I already knew that.

"It doesn't sound too bad so far," I summarized, eyeing her as she sipped at her wine. "Now, for the other side of the coin. What didn't you like?" I steeled myself, knowing I had to listen to her critique without charging over there and forcing Tiffany to rescind her account from her knees.

She swallowed, conveying her own nervousness.

"I didn't like that you sedated me, Master." Her gaze lifted to mine. "You had no right to do that."

Holding my free palm up in a gesture of conciliation, I nodded. "You're correct. It was unnecessary, and I apologize."

The oddest part was, as the words left my lips, I might have actually meant them. I'd spent months cultivating the perfect plan to capture and use Tiffany but had given virtually no thought to her feelings. Assured by her passion for humiliation and objectification, I was so damn sure she'd come on board, so certain I could twist her desire into obedience, I hadn't considered her responses beyond that. She had been a wonderful aesthetic, a litany of gorgeous holes to fuck —it was easy to dehumanize her.

Sitting with Tiffany now, the whole woman was even easier to fall for. Sure, I would use and torment her, but for some peculiar reason, I was enjoying this time. I needed to know her opinions, to take them on board when I finally got my hands on her.

"Well, thank you." She was taken aback by my contrition.

"What else?" I prompted. "Let's address everything, shall we?"

She nodded slowly. "I hated that you hid in my house."

Naturally, I had expected that protest.

"It still makes me feel sick to know you were there all that time." She shivered.

"I didn't hurt you, little girl. I would never harm you."

"But still…" She inhaled. "It's such a violation."

"I accept that." Lifting my glass to my lips, I sipped the full-bodied red. "But I'm not sorry for all the time I had to get to know you. It meant I could give you everything you needed."

Tiffany's eyes widened.

"All those dark fantasies…"

Her gaze fluttered closed, and she gripped the stem of her glass.

"It's like you can see into my soul."

"That's the point," I reiterated. "I know you so well, I practically can."

A weighted silence bloomed between us. I watched her compose herself, sipping at her wine before she found the right words.

"You can be so cruel sometimes, Master."

My lips curled. I had been expecting this one, too.

"Like when?"

Of course, there were numerous examples she could offer, but I sought to know precisely what she had in mind. What one thing, in all the myriad of discomfiture and mortification she'd endured, stood out in her mind.

"Like all those horrible orgasms." She screwed her face into a ball at the memory.

"Too much pleasure?" My tone was sardonic. "That's an unusual complaint."

"It was awful." Her voice was hushed. "I thought I was going to pass out."

"You did pass out," I reminded her. "And you survived."

Her face blanched as she exhaled. "I still didn't enjoy it, Master."

"Duly noted." Noted but not a promise to refrain from delivering forced orgasms in the future. Sometimes, they were exactly what a little girl like Tiffany required to remind her who was in charge. Similarly, denial was also an effective tool of control.

As if she read my mind, she went on. "Taking me right to the edge, then not letting me come." Her expression crumpled. "That was mean, as well."

"You like it when I'm mean." It was fun playing with her again, watching her finger the stem of her glass as she grappled for composure. "You like it a lot."

"I…" Her free hand rose to her temple. "I know. That's why it's so confusing."

Leaning toward her, I wanted to bound past the sleek coffee table and take her hand. Yes, I wanted to rip her clothes off, but more than that, I wanted to reassure her. I had to let Tiffany know she was mine—in every single regard—which meant nurture as well as coercion.

"I'm sorry you're confused." I set my glass on the table, meeting her puzzled expression. "Why don't I make things clearer?"

CHAPTER 17: TIFFANY

My head was spinning. I still didn't know if coming here had been the biggest mistake of my life or the beginning of the most wondrous adventure. I barely knew what I wanted. One thing was for certain, I could never explain this to Melissa or the police. Aside from the authorities, my friend was the only one who knew about my ordeal. She'd replied to the message I'd sent before Kade had crashed into my consciousness, and I'd reached out from the hospital once he'd fled the scene. She'd witnessed my tears and angst. She knew some of the things I'd suffered at Kade's hands but would never understand why I had responded to him. Hell, *I* didn't even completely understand it.

"How can you make it clearer, Master?" I asked, aware he was eyeing my every move. I shifted in my seat, conscious that every time I addressed him as my master, my core temperature rose. The room was so hot, whereas five minutes before, I'd been comfortable. It was perturbing.

"Well," he started, pressing his elbows into his suit pants as he leaned in my direction. He looked devilishly handsome.

"We talked about what you liked and what you didn't. How about we discuss the most important thing?" He paused, his stare drilling into me, prompting me to speak.

"Wh-What's that, Master?"

Kade flashed me one of his perfect smiles, the type a shark might offer a small fish before it gobbled them up. The analogy did little to quell my rising nervous energy.

"What you *want*, little girl."

The muscles at the apex of my sex clenched.

"I-I don't know." That was precisely the point. I adored so much about the enigmatic stranger who'd torn into my mundane life and thrown everything on its head, but I couldn't abide his style or the way he had no qualms about what he'd done. How could I reconcile that?

"Yes, you do." He was so damn self-assured. "You just haven't admitted it to yourself yet." His lips twitched. "It's like the kinky sex and humiliation play, little girl." A dark glint shone in his gray gaze. "You know you want it, but you're too afraid—or ashamed—to say so."

My lips parted at his accurate analysis, my mind blown that this man, who I hardly knew, could read me so well.

"So, I say this," Kade continued. "The time for fear and shame is over."

My brow rose, and he chuckled.

"For the time being, at least," he clarified with a smirk. "Be honest with me about what you desire, but more importantly, be honest with yourself."

"It's not that easy." Playing with my wine glass, I was suddenly absurdly self-conscious. Not that it made any sense. Kade was a man who had seen me at my very worst and witnessed my most embarrassing moments. Hell, he'd bloody recorded most of them. Why was I uncomfortable now? "It's not as easy as just giving in to my desires, Master."

"Why isn't it?" His dark eyebrow rose, mocking me. "What could be easier, little girl?"

"I have a life." For the first time since he'd seized me, I was in a position to spell it out for Kade. "A career I enjoy and a life I am building. Being your full-time thrall isn't conducive with those things." I paused to catch my breath, aware of how hard I'd been breathing as I stated my case.

"My thrall?" He ran his tongue over his teeth. "Now, that's a wonderful thought, little girl."

"Please." I swallowed. "Don't tease me. I hope you can understand what I'm saying."

"I'm not teasing." He rose from his place, taking a stride in my direction. Shocked by his sudden move, as though I could possibly have forgotten how tall he was, I reeled back, almost emptying the contents of my glass over the couch.

"Careful." Kade swooped, rescuing my glass and guiding it to the coffee table to join his. "Are you okay?"

It seemed such a preposterous thing to ask. After everything he'd put me through, now he was worried that I was all right?

"Yes." I nodded. "Thank you."

"May I?" He gestured to the seat beside me.

I could tell how much effort it was taking for him to play the gentleman. Kade was far more used to getting what he wanted without inquiry.

Taking in the cut of his expensive suit, I breathed in his spicy cologne. The scent washed over me, bringing flashes from our time at the house—vivid memories of me bound to the bed, crying out as I climaxed, and the heady sensation that had overawed when he'd finally screwed me and given us both what we'd wanted. I gulped at the realization. We *had* both wanted that, and it had been incredible.

"Yes, of course." I inched over, making room for him as he sat beside me.

"Yes, little girl." His voice was solemn. "Yes, I understand the point you're making, but maybe this doesn't have to be about absolutes." His brows knitted as though he couldn't believe he was admitting it.

"How do you mean, Master?" Had I ever been this close to him before without him fondling and coaxing me? Had I ever just looked into those huge silver eyes and spoken to him?

"I managed our introduction the way I deal with most things." He smirked.

"Like a bull in a china shop?" I proffered, blushing as I realized what had just escaped my mouth.

"Watch it, little girl." His tone was playful as he leaned closer, and while he didn't touch me, his face was so close, our lips almost grazed. A guttural moan stirred in my throat at his proximity, and I regretted his vow not to make physical contact until I asked for it. I wanted Kade to do what Kade did—take control and take the kiss we both so badly wanted.

"I'm sorry." I dropped my gaze. "That wasn't very diplomatic."

"No," he agreed. "Don't stop looking at me. If I can't touch you. I want to see you."

My focus flitted back to him in a heartbeat.

"Better." He smiled. "I only meant I could ease up a little." He inhaled as if the point was painful. "Give you more of the balance you need, so long as you're mine."

"Balance?"

The passion burning in his gaze was making it impossible to think, as was his final word that kept bouncing around my head like a pop song stuck on repeat.

Mine. Mine. Mine.

"Yes," he purred. "You could work, so long as you don't

work too much. All those long hours are bad for you, little girl. I'm there to ensure you do a better job."

"You'd let me work?" Wait, why was I asking? I didn't need Kade's permission to move forward in the profession I'd been engaged in for more than a decade. I didn't need anyone's permission. How had this hurricane of a man blown into my life and conditioned me to this way of thinking?

Because it's not all him, is it?

I blinked as the unhelpful voice bleated a response in my mind.

You've always wanted this, Tiff. You wanted a man to take control, to prop you up and make rules for you to follow. It's more than only about sex. It's always been more.

"Yes." There was that amazing smile again, the one that dazzled and splintered my thought process. "If we agree to terms that satisfy me, I am prepared to compromise for what I want." Once again, his expression was stunned by his admission.

"For what you want, Master?" I gazed at him, looking for something more than the sizzling desire I knew waited there —clarification, reassurance, something with substance.

"For you." He shifted closer, tilting his head, and for one glorious moment, I thought he would put us both out of our misery and just fucking kiss me. "I want *you*, little girl. In my life and at my feet."

Fuck, he made that sound so good. Too good.

"I want that, too." Had I said that out loud… to the man who thought it was acceptable to sneak around my house and record me? "I just don't know how it would work, balancing a semblance of my old life with you, Master."

"We never know until we make it work." His lips curled. "Until we try. Are you prepared to try, Tiffany?"

Christ, the way he said my name was electrifying.

"Yes." The word was out of my mouth before I had time to process its meaning. "Yes, Master, I want to try."

At that moment, I couldn't envision a world without him. As sick as it sounded, I didn't want that world. Kade had tormented and degraded me, tethered and exposed me without permission. He'd wielded power over me like a god, but when push came to shove, he had been true to his word. He never hurt me beyond the pinch of a nipple clamp or the sting of his palm. He never endangered my life—I had been the one who brandished a weapon to his throat. I panted at the unwelcome memory.

"What is it?" His warm breath tickled my skin, taunting me.

"I was just thinking..." I hesitated. "We haven't exactly had the most conventional start have we, Master?"

"That's true." Kade chuckled. "But I've never much been one for convention, little girl."

Smiling, I dwelled on every moment of his lack of conformity. I'd loathed the things he'd done, but Kade had taken me higher than anyone else ever had. I wanted those highs as much as I wanted to lead in court or top up my personal pension. I deserved the pleasure only he could deliver.

"I can imagine, Master."

"What else do you want?" He pinioned me with his mesmerizing gaze. "Apart from balance, what else would make you happy?"

"The respect I talked about before."

Christ, I was going to explode if he didn't touch me soon. I knew he was waiting for me to invite him—as he'd promised—but I missed his urgency, the primal need in his every caress. I missed the edge that made Kade so fucking irresistible.

"Define respect."

"I mean, if I have something to say, I'd like to be listened to." I sensed the heat pooling in my cheeks and knew I was blushing. "I'd like to think you were interested in what I have to say."

"Oh, I am, little girl." His lips lowered to my nape, and reflexively, my eyes flitted closed, but to my disappointment, it was his voice that continued, not his kisses. "You fascinate me, and I'm enjoying just talking." His lips curled as he straightened. "We will have those times. Times when we talk, when we touch base to see if the other is happy." His gaze held mine knowingly. "But don't think for a moment that I won't gag that pretty little mouth when you need it."

Oh God.

My lips parted, though I had nothing sensible to say.

"When you need me to take control and use you."

"Kade." His name slipped from me. "Master, please." I was going to ignite if he didn't cater to my needs soon.

"What?" His conceited smirk told me he knew exactly what my problem was, but he was going to torment me the way he always had. He would make me say it aloud. "What do you need?"

"You." A raspy urgency radiated in my voice.

"What can I do, little girl?" That tantalizing eyebrow arched again. "I told you I wouldn't touch you without your say so."

Shit, it all came down to this—this heady precipice where I had to cede and tell him what I wanted.

"I need you to touch me… please." Brushing my mouth over his, I groaned as he responded, his lips kissing me back and delivering the dominance I craved. "Please, I've missed you." It was the most dangerous statement I'd ever made, but the truth rushed from my mouth between caresses as Kade pushed his weight against me.

"I missed you too, little girl." His hands were on me, over me, everywhere.

I moaned as one snaked around me while another tightened in my tresses. Easing me back onto the sofa, he pressed gentle kisses to my chin before dipping to my neck. "So. Fucking. Much."

"Master." My eyes closed at the sheer exhilaration of his touch. "What's going to happen?"

"You're going to get everything you've ever wanted, little girl." There wasn't a flicker of doubt in his tone. "Your master will give you the world."

CHAPTER 18: KADE

What was I doing, promising her the world? This wasn't about her. It had never been about anyone but me—my unrelenting needs, my irrefutable desire—but that was bullshit. It wasn't about me —it was all about Tiffany. She was the one who'd captivated me, who'd changed my frame of reference. The woman in my arms was the reason I no longer had to kill to satiate my need. She was everything.

That's why I made the vow, and staring down at her awestruck face, I realized that was why I'd stand by it.

"I don't know what to say, Master." Huge blue eyes bored into me as I dragged her wrists over her head and pinned them there.

"The time for speaking is over."

My words were an edict in the new order burgeoning between us. I had meant what I said. I would compromise, would make time for her to talk, tell me about her fears and dreams, and let her continue her work. The last commitment tore at me the greatest.

Allowing her to leave and go back to the drudgery she

called a profession gnawed, but I would discover a way to make it palatable. Perhaps dictating her attire, more specifically what she wore beneath it, would help to take the edge off while she had to leave my side.

I grinned at the idea, my cock thickening as it tried to bury itself into her hip. I would also have strict rules about the hours she was permitted to work and magnificent punishments lined up for potential failures. I couldn't fucking wait.

"I need you out of these clothes." My eyes fell to her t-shirt.

"Yes, Master." Her voice was heavy with trepidation, but I heard the arousal as well. She was scared, understandably so, but excited enough to suppress the fear. I adored that about Tiffany. That was the tiny bud in her I would help blossom.

Rising from her body, I helped her to her feet, then took a seat once more as she shuffled out of her clothing. My ardor intensified exponentially as she discarded the clothes at her feet, finally slipping out of her white cotton underwear. There wouldn't be any such lingerie in Tiffany's possession once I was done with her. That much, I could guarantee.

"Beautiful." I drank her in, enjoying the curve of her hips and the swell of her breasts. She was even better than I remembered... and I *had* remembered. "Now kneel."

Breath ragged, she fell to her knees before me, her gaze lowering.

"Did you miss this, little girl?" My cock strained to be free as I hooked one finger under her chin, compelling her gaze back to me.

"Yes, Master."

Mettle reverberated in her reply, a tone I hadn't heard before. Tiffany was resolved to be there with me... on her knees. Triumph soared, an acknowledgment of how much her consent meant.

I'd always wondered what difference would consensus make. Would it change something in my head? Detract from the thrill? Looking into her incredible blue eyes, the answer was abundantly obvious. It was different because she chose to be there and a thousand times better than before. Tiffany's agreement was a gift, a precious honor I would have to work to keep. It was a challenge I was determined to rise to.

As if the organ understood my consideration, my erection throbbed impatiently, demanding I take more of what we both wanted from this delicate new arrangement.

"Know what I require from you next?"

Her gaze flitted to my lap, the corners of her mouth twitching.

"Not until you tell me, Master."

"Good answer, little girl." Stroking the underside of her jaw, my hand slid into her hair. "But I think you were right the first time." My free hand moved to my zipper, freeing my impatient cock, which leapt out as if it also wanted to show her how missed she had been. "Polish this for me. I want to see you choking on it before I empty my load over your gorgeous face."

Tiffany bit back on her smile as she shifted on her knees, settling into a comfortable position. "It would be my pleasure, Master."

"Recall where your hands should go?" I smoothed her hair back as she slid her wrists to the small of her back.

"Like this, Master?"

"Wonderful," I praised. "I'll find some binds for you, but for now, let me just enjoy you." Pressing gently at the back of her head, I guided her to my eager dick, exhaling as she wrapped her lips around my crown.

"Yes." Digits stiffening in her hair, I directed her down to the base, groaning as she struggled with my excited length. "Perfect." Fisting her hair, I steered her up and down my shaft, relishing the exquisite sensation as her throat ceded to my will. Tears brimmed in her eyes as she grappled with its unyielding demand, but to her credit, never once did she try to rise, move, or protest.

"No wonder you missed this," I growled, increasing her pace with my fist. "When this is what you're fucking made for."

Tiffany's attention darted to me, tear-stained lashes blinking rapidly as my cock took what it wanted.

"That's right." I was close to climax as I elaborated. "That's why you came back, isn't it?" My balls tightened at the gurgling noises coming from her mouth. "Because you know what you're good for, what your purpose is?" Shifting closer, I lunged into her throat. "Answer me!"

"E-es, Aster," she spluttered around my hard length.

"I knew it."

Reaching forward, I held her head with both hands as I drove between her lips. I wasn't gentle as I took what was mine, not wanting there to be any illusions that our reconciliation meant I would be soft and easy. Tiffany was back because she knew what she wanted and knew I could satisfy those needs. In turn, I fully intended to, which meant treating her like the dumb whore she needed to morph into to create the fireworks in her mind.

I'd been wrong before, assuming she could be that objectified persona full time, but her break for freedom had taught me it wasn't enough, not for a woman as intoxicating as mine. She needed both the excitement of my possession, the thrill of her submission, and the consistency of the career she'd started. If I wanted to keep her, I would have to see to all her needs.

"Take it, little girl." My voice was a low snarl as I neared ecstasy. "Take it all."

I cried out as the first wave of pleasure drowned me, pulling away with a trail of her saliva. Positioning my cock over her face, I pumped my seed into her open mouth. Tiffany, like the good little girl she was, waited on her knees as I milked my cum between her lips. The sense of release was as palpable as it was exquisite as I crashed back against the leather sofa.

"That's better." I blew out a breath as I met her eyes. "We're both back where we should be."

She smiled, collecting the remnants of my cum with her supple tongue.

"Yes, Master."

"I'm glad we agree, little girl." Leaning toward her, I beckoned her to my lap. She straddled me as I tugged her closer. Her tantalizing assets grazed my shirt as I squeezed her delectable backside.

"Master." Her voice was like a sigh.

"Hmmm?"

"Thank you."

"What are you thanking me for, little girl?" I pulled her against me, widening my stance so her thighs were forced to spread. The hand on her ass slipped between her legs, my fingertips grazing over her tempting pussy. *My* pussy.

"Listening to me." Her breaths came hard and fast as I explored what was mine. "Allowing me to speak."

"Of course." I smiled, finding her clit and circling the small ball of nerves until she gasped. "I will ensure we have that time." Sliding my finger back, I dipped it between her labia, awed by how excited her delicious cunt was. "You shall also fulfill your professional commitments."

"I can't believe it." She groaned, her eyes fluttering closed as I pushed my digit into her core. "It's more than I could have imagined, Master."

"Get used to it, little girl," I purred. "You'll be legal eagle by day and my little cumslut by night." I grinned when her hips rocked forward, pushing back against my finger. "What are you doing? Are you pleasuring yourself on your master's finger?"

"Oh God," she panted. "Yes, Master. I'm sorry."

"You're not sorry," I chided playfully. I stared into her eyes as I rewarded her with a second digit. "The sooner I get you plugged and gagged again, the better."

"Yes, Master." She was lost to the rhythm of my hand, her back arching as she rode my digits.

"Tell me," I demanded, using her juices to lubricate her tight little asshole. Slipping another finger into her rectum, my recently satiated cock roused at her carnal cry. "Tell me how much you need to be gagged and plugged. Tell me whose cumslut you are, and you can have your pleasure."

"Yes, Master." She thrust her tits into me as she rocked on my fingers. "I need all those things. I need to be plugged and gagged for you."

Reaching around her head, I tugged her hair, compelling her into a harder arch. "You forgot the most important part," I admonished. "Whose whore are you, little girl? Who do you belong to?"

She clenched around my fingers, gasping as her pleasure peaked.

"You, Master," she screamed. "I belong to you."

Collapsing against him, I buried my face into his crisp linen shirt as my lips stretched wide with hedonism.

"Fuck!" I snugged into his hard body, gasping as his hand slipped from my hair to cradle the back of my head.

This was why I could never walk away from Kade, why I'd answered his damn messages and came calling at his request. It might not be the best reason to return to the man who'd captured you, wasn't sane, and probably shouldn't be the basis of any romantic entanglement, but it was worth it. At this moment, it was all I needed. I'd never known passion like it and wasn't prepared to do without.

"Thank you, Master." I offered the gratitude before he could demand it, his soft chuckle more than enough reward.

"You're welcome." Leaning forward, he pressed a kiss into my crown as his other hand slid from my spasming pussy. "I want you to remember something."

Glancing up into his brooding face, I met his gray gaze. "What, Master."

"What you already admitted." He grinned. "That you belong to me."

Amid the frenzy of our carnal union, there seemed little doubt. Not so long ago, I had been Kade's prisoner, but he hadn't forced me into anything since I came to his suite. The only thing keeping me there now was his enthralling smile and the promise of all the pleasure we'd create together.

I was a captive of my desire.

"That this belongs to me." His hand squeezed my labia lightly before brushing between my cheeks to my ass. "And this."

My nipples beaded at his possessive tone. It made no sense to find it alluring. Kade was a dark god who'd been sent to entrance me, and I no longer had the will to resist.

"I won't forget, Master."

Holding my gaze, he pulled me closer, and for one lingering moment, we simply gazed at each other. It was impossible to say what I saw blazing in his eyes. They smoldered with an intensity I'd never known, thick evocative smoke that cleared to reveal flickers of humanity he hadn't shown me before. Staring into them, I could almost believe he felt something more for me, affection that went beyond lust and bodily fluids, but—

A sudden vibration at the end of the couch splintered the burgeoning intimacy, and our attention was drawn to my phone, buzzing on the arm of the sofa.

"Expecting a call?"

"No, Master." My heart raced at his wry tone, but his arm softened on my waist, releasing me to take the call. Sliding from his lap, I reached for the device, my brow furrowing. "Oh God, it's one of the detectives who've been questioning me."

"Answer it." His lips curled.

"B-But?" I stammered. "It's the police."

"And you have nothing to hide." His gaze drilled into me. "If you don't answer, they'll be suspicious."

"Oh, crap." I knew he was right, but I couldn't bring myself to answer the damn call.

"Here." Grasping the device, Kade accepted the incoming call before thrusting the phone back into my hands. Shell-shocked, my gaze slid from him to the screen, realizing I would have to speak.

"Miss Noble?"

I could hear DS Lucas on the other end as I lifted the device to my ear.

"Hi." Closing my eyes, I tried to will Kade away as I feigned normalcy, but it was impossible. I sensed him there, whether or not I saw him.

"Are you okay?" Lucas already sounded skeptical. "You sound breathless?"

Perfect.

"Yeah, I was in the bathroom when you called." My eyes opened with the lie, meeting Kade's knowing gaze. "I just caught you."

"Oh, I'm sorry for the interruption," Lucas went on. "I just wanted to check in with you after your rather abrupt exit this morning. How are you feeling now?"

"I'm fine, just tired." Turning on the couch, I perched on the edge of the seat.

"Tired of our questions?" she asked sardonically.

"Yes, actually." My tone hardened. "This whole thing has been a nightmare, and having to constantly relive each moment with you and DC Granger isn't helping."

Kade shifted in my peripheral vision, rising to his full height as I tried to concentrate on Lucas' response.

"I understand, Miss Noble, but you'll appreciate this is part of the course."

Glancing in Kade's direction, I noticed he'd discarded his shirt, revealing his muscular pectorals and honed obliques. The man was distracting, to say the least. I watched as he fastened his pants, my eyes rising to his smug smirk.

"… sure you understand why."

I tuned back into Lucas' voice too late, missing most of her sentence.

"Yes, of course." Flustering, my mind raced as I tried to improvise. "But I'm going to need some time."

"How much time?" Her tone was clipped as if she knew what was really going on.

"I don't know." My tone was defensive. "As much as I need."

"You realize there is no case without you, Tiffany?" Lucas sighed. "Has something happened I need to know about?"

"No," I answered at once. "As I said, I'm fine, but I can't live like this anymore. I need some space. In fact, I'm thinking of taking a holiday."

Kade folded his arms across his broad chest, his lips twitching.

"A holiday?" Lucas spat. "Now?"

"Now seems like the perfect time." Inhaling, I relaxed back in my chair. "I've had a stressful week, Detective. I'm sure you can understand."

"I do, but a vacation wouldn't be my recommendation at this moment."

Her tone was decidedly sterner, which only hardened my resolve. I'd had just about enough of everyone making choices for me. I'd only just worked through some of Kade's control issues, and I still had Rex to deal with at work. The last thing I needed was the authorities on my back as well. It had to stop.

"Duly noted, Detective." I met Kade's gaze, aware I was repeating his earlier response. His dark brow rose as if he had noticed. "But I believe it is my choice, not yours."

"Well, yes, but…" Lucas' voice prattled on, but I tuned out, focusing on the more than six feet of man crouched in front of me. Lifting his hand, he signaled for me to wrap up the call, and my heart raced.

"Is there anything else, Detective?" I cut Lucas off mid-sentence. "Because I need to rest."

"Are you saying you want to drop the charges, Miss Noble? We had assumed your cooperation."

I couldn't help but smile at her gruff tone, my gaze lowering as I fought to compose myself. It wouldn't do to laugh while she was on the other end of the line.

"I'm saying I want time, Detective." The lawyer in me sprang to life, avoiding her question. "And it's my right to demand it."

"Understood." She inhaled, and I imagined her features puckered in disgust. "Though I would remind you, we could prosecute you for wasting police time."

"Is that a threat?" I snorted, rising to my feet.

Kade craned his head to watch as I strode toward the door and paced. Anger reared inside me with each step. Who the hell did Lucas think she was? I was the fucking victim in this case, and if I wasn't comfortable to proceed, she should offer reassurance and support, not wield threats she had no leverage to back up. No wonder so many cases never made it to court. The police were bloody useless.

"I'd think very carefully before you continue, Detective."

"Not at all." She forced a laugh. "I was merely stating the facts as I see them, Miss Noble."

"You don't have any facts without me."

"We have the footage from the cameras the perpetrator left on your property."

My heart pounded faster at the reminder of all the deeply personal things Lucas and her colleagues had seen since I'd called the police.

"You have neither a suspect in custody nor a victim, Detective. The Crown Prosecution Service won't touch this case with a barge pole."

Strained silence filled the line as I tried to steady my breathing. Turning, I caught sight of Kade's lips stretching into a smirk. He was sprawled out on the sofa, an odd glint in his eyes. I swallowed, realizing what the twinkle reminded me of—pride. He was proud of me.

"It seems we have an impasse." I blew out a breath, anxious to finish the call.

"Indeed." Lucas' reply was curt. "We'll be in touch, Miss Noble."

I closed my eyes as the call ended, pulling in a replenishing breath before my gaze opened.

"Well, well, well, little girl," Kade smirked. "I never knew you were such a good liar."

"I'm a lawyer, Master." I shrugged. "Manipulating the truth comes with the territory."

"Come here." He beckoned me with his palm. "Sounds like we need to plan a holiday?"

Relaxing, I walked to him.

"I only said that to throw her off the scent," I explained, falling to my knees.

My brow creased as my knees grazed the carpet. I'd knelt, and he hadn't even told me to. Why? Reaching for his shin, I buried my face into his thigh as the answer hit me. I knelt because that's where I wanted to be, where I found serenity. Fuck, how messed up was that? I didn't know if I was lost or found. As his hand settled in my hair, all I knew was Kade—and whatever this visceral madness was between us—had become the insanity that was keeping me sane.

"Happy down there, little girl?" His tone was playful as he ruffled my hair.

"Yes, Master." Smiling against his expensive suit, I no longer tried to reconcile the why or the how. I was happy, content to just be. For the first time in an age, my thoughts weren't scattered—worried about a case or whether Rex would let me lead. I was centered and whole, as though my submission had grounded me. "I am."

"You're amazing."

I lifted my chin to see him smile.

"Why, Master?" I asked, still clinging to his leg.

"You're so multi-faceted and complex, I'd never noticed before."

"You only saw me as a thing you could objectify. I suppose you'd never seen me at work."

"You're right." His hand slid to the side of my face, stroking my cheek. "Believe me, I will still objectify you, but now I see you also need an avenue for this other side of you."

A memory of me as his footrest burst into my mind, and my lips twitched at the sizzling recollection. I might have fought to be free, but there was no denying I had loved being used that way.

"Thinking about how I objectified you?" He laughed, the deep throaty sound that seemed to speak directly to my clitoris.

"Yes, Master." Was I so transparent?

"Don't worry, little girl. There'll be much more of that."

Apprehensive excitement furled in my belly. How was it

possible to be simultaneously filled with dread and eagerness for the same outcome?

"But that doesn't mean I don't respect the lawyer in you." He shifted forward. "I'd like to see you in action in court sometime."

Him and me both.

"I'm not sure how easy that will be, Master, but..." I smiled, imagining the scene. "I'd like that, too."

"Do you need to call work before we continue?" Those gray eyes drilled into me.

"No, I..." I hesitated, recalling the agonizing conversations I'd shared with Rex the last few days. "I've taken some time off." It was strange saying it. I couldn't remember the last time I'd taken annual leave.

Kade's brow furrowed. "How much time?"

"It's flexible," I explained. "A week for now, but there's more if I want it."

"So, we could take that holiday?" That teasing eyebrow cocked.

"I guess." I pulled in a breath, unable to envision holidaying with the man who'd imprisoned and ignited me. I didn't know if I would ever get over the fiend Kade had been when we'd first met, but I could no longer deny the way he made me feel. He gave me a reason I couldn't ignore or had the will to try. Whatever dark path Kade was leading me down was the one I'd chosen. "What did you have in mind, Master?"

"Some time away with my new cumslut."

The butterflies in my tummy scattered as his gaze flashed with nefarious intent.

"Wh-Where, Master?"

Crap. How did he make everything sound so fucking enticing? That was Kade's gift. He took the inoffensive and twisted it into perverted magic. Staring into his eyes, I realized I was panting, needing to know more.

"Wherever I say." His lips curled. "That's the beauty of this arrangement, little girl. I lead, and you follow, preferably leashed and on your hands and knees."

Catching my lip between my teeth, I remembered how terrifying it had been to be led around my house. Terrifying and demeaning, yet everything I had fantasized about for years.

"We can't stay here for long," he pondered out loud. "My suite is secure, but the police will follow you and will soon discover you're no longer frequenting Room 725."

My brows knitted. "How did you know my room number, Master?" I had been meaning to ask since we'd met again. "How did you know where to send the flowers?"

"I have my ways, little girl." He chuckled darkly. "You know that."

"You were watching me?" Again. I shivered at the prospect, already knowing in my heart it was true. I wasn't sure how, but I sensed Kade had reverted to form. He wanted me back, so he'd used his trademark ingenuity to ensure it transpired.

"Yes, I was watching you." His gaze drilled into my face. "Did you really think I'd just let you go?"

"No, I..." My throat dried as I tried to articulate my thoughts, but I didn't know how to rationalize what he was telling me. I hadn't expected Kade to change, especially in such a short time, but the idea he'd tracked me to this hotel and waited for the opportunity to pounce was disconcerting.

"What?" He reached for my hair, fisting it roughly. "What did you think?"

"I don't know, Master." I gasped as electricity fired at my scalp. "I was in shock and didn't know what to think."

His hand relaxed a fraction. "We didn't exactly part on the best terms."

"No," I croaked, conscious of who had initiated the abrupt separation. I didn't regret calling for help—I'd needed it—but Kade's inference was right. The sudden severance had given us no time to reconcile the twisted deeds that had taken place.

"Do you want to know what I did while we were apart?" Sincerity burned in his eyes. "In the spirit of transparency, I will tell you… everything."

My throat dried at the caution vibrating in his voice. Inadvertent or not, it warned me that proceeding would mean discovering things I wouldn't appreciate.

"I don't know, Master." I rose to my knees and moved closer, no longer worried I was naked while he was clothed. In fact, I rather liked the distinction. Being with Kade allowed me to unleash the woman I'd suppressed all those years. The submissive, decadent side of me wanted nothing more than to kneel and degrade herself because she found freedom in the exchange. I liked that woman. I'd never given her a chance. "Do I want to know?"

"You're a smart woman, little girl." He flashed a mischievous grin. "That's for you to decide. I choose what happens next. You get to select what you want to know about your master."

Jesus, when he put it like that, I didn't know what to think, but gazing into his handsome profile, there really was only one choice.

"I'd like to know, Master."

His lips twitched. "Of course, you do." He patted his lap. "Up here, little girl. We need another heart-to-heart."

Climbing onto his lap, my pulse quickened. I was vividly aware Kade was going to tell me something I didn't want to hear but conscious that this was who he was. Even if I hadn't known the details, I'd understood the nature of the devil and been under no illusions. I was a big girl, and after everything he'd put me through at the house, I knew what I was getting into.

"I'm ready, Master." Straddling him, I realized I was.

CHAPTER 20: KADE

Pride bloomed in my chest as I watched Tiffany dispatch the hapless detective. I hadn't seen this side of her before, but I liked what I witnessed. Yes, that woman wasn't as sexy as the naked one who wanted to curl up at my feet or the one I intended to tether and command, but she was something else—a strong and capable woman I hadn't known existed until today. This new aspect of Tiffany only fueled my passion for her. The knowledge I would conquer not only the slut between the sheets but also the attorney with strength and prowess was exciting.

I hadn't intended to steer the conversation from that sense of pride. There was no plan to open my heart and divulge all the insidious ways I had hunted her, but now that she was wrapped around me, the intoxicating scent of her hair wafting on my nostrils, I found I didn't care. Let there be honesty. Let all our cards be on the table. Tiffany might as well know the monster she'd chosen, and like it or not, she *had* chosen me. Capturing her in the attic had been the genesis of our connection, but the primal urge that allowed it to bloom was just as much her choice as mine.

Sure, I'd have seized what I wanted regardless, taken her if she'd resisted, but it meant something that she'd selected me, stirring me unexpectedly. I found I wanted to cherish her as well as crush, protect her as well as pulverize, and for the first time, the idea didn't perturb. Now that I'd found her again, I wasn't letting her go.

"I'm ready, Master." Resolve echoed in her voice as her gaze settled on me.

"Are you sure? You might not like what you hear."

"I'm sure." She nodded. "What happened?"

"I fled the house." I inhaled, mentally reliving the moment I'd assaulted the incompetent cop and found freedom. "But I was in freefall. It took me a while to put all the pieces together."

"Pieces?" She shifted on my lap, stirring my ever-hungry cock.

"Of what had happened." I absently trailed a finger over her shoulder. "One moment, you were my fabulous footrest, and the next, the police were at the door."

"Oh."

She squirmed, clearly remembering who had been responsible for the authorities' arrival, but I meant what I'd texted. I wasn't in this for revenge, and if her intervention had accidentally allowed this new intimacy, I was glad. One thing was for sure, I would never have permitted her to speak at the house. I'd been in a haze of dark-filled desire, and compromise wasn't one of them.

"I found somewhere away from the house to check the footage I'd taken of you."

Her cheeks reddened as she listened.

"That's where I discovered what you'd done." I couldn't hide the hurt in my voice. Maybe I had no right to feel betrayed, but I struggled with the emotion, nonetheless.

Tiffany's eyes fluttered closed for a moment. "I can't say I'm sorry, Master." She blew out a breath. "If that's what you're waiting for."

"I could make you." I leaned closer, relishing the way her eyes widened at my deeper tone. "I could push you right back to the brink and demand an apology."

"I know." Her voice was breathless. "But if you did, you'd know I didn't mean it. The contrition would only be offered under duress."

"Duress?" I chuckled. "You're making it sound even hotter, little girl."

Her lips curled. "Not intentionally, Master. Like you said, I'm trying to be honest."

She was a revelation. A woman attractive enough to keep me hard, who was simultaneously smart and submissive. I was lucky to have found her but to have tempted her back was beyond good fortune. As she writhed on top of me, I wondered just how deep this rabbit hole would go. Was it possible for a man like me—a brute who had enjoyed snuffing out so many beautiful lights in the past—to feel anything? Was the tug I'd experienced when we were apart only lust and the sting of loss, or could I possibly be falling for the tantalizing brunette?

"Good." My hand rose to her nape, pulling her so close, our noses grazed. "Let's keep it that way."

"I wouldn't dare to lie to you, Master."

She grinned, and I had the sense she was playing, but oddly, it didn't bother me. I had her—on my lap, naked and willing—more than I could have hoped.

"Back to my story." I skimmed my lips over hers, considering forgetting the retelling altogether and just fucking her.

"What did you think when you saw what I'd done,

Master?" She inhaled, her beading nipples grazing the hair on my chest.

"I was disappointed."

Tiffany looked crestfallen, though she surely must have guessed my response.

"But I started to understand." My tone softened. "As the hours turned into days, I cared less about what you'd done and more about getting you back. After all, it wasn't the first time you'd hurt me." My hand rose to my neck, brushing over the scar her blade had left.

"Oh God." She sighed. "I was a bitch to you, Master."

"Because I pressed all of your buttons without asking your view." I laughed gently at the memory. "I provoked you." It was the closest thing Tiffany would get to a sorry.

"Yes, but still..." She shook her head. "I resorted to violence." Her gaze fixed on the injury she'd inflicted, her hand rising toward it. "May I, Master?"

"You want to touch it?" My tone was sardonic.

"Please."

"Go on then." Tilting my head, I exposed my neck, watching as she leaned toward it. Her expression crumpled as she examined the remnants of her outburst. She recoiled, clearly more disappointed in herself than I could ever be.

"I'm sorry, Master." She met my eyes. "It doesn't matter what you did. You never took a knife to me." Her gaze welled with tears. "I shouldn't have cut you."

"As I see it, little girl, your mistake wasn't the knife." I captured her small hand, entwining our fingers as I went on. "It was not having the balls to use it."

"What?" Her lips parted. "You're saying I didn't cut your throat properly, Master?"

"I'm saying if you wield a weapon, you should be ready to use it, but in the end, you weren't, were you?"

"No." A solitary tear fell from her eye.

Releasing her hand, I caught it with my thumb.

"I didn't really want to kill you. I just wanted it to stop."

"You wanted what to stop?"

"Your relentlessness." She gasped, tucking the loose strands of her hair behind her ear. "The fact I couldn't think straight. I didn't know how to respond to your treatment."

"Your body did," I reminded, as my erection swelled beneath her.

"Yes," she agreed with a half-smile. "But I am more than only my body."

"Yes, you are," I concurred, brushing my lips over her forehead. "You're my cumslut with a sharp wit and a shrewd mind."

She laughed.

"What did you do next, Master? How did you come to be in this suite?"

"It wasn't difficult. When I discovered you hadn't returned to the house, I found out where the police had put you."

"The hotel?" Her brows knitted, but she fought to smooth the gesture.

Clearly, the fact I could trace her whereabouts still agitated her, but as with everything that had happened between us, Tiffany was torn. She loathed my insistence, and no doubt found it unnerving, but she was glad I'd found her. I could see how troublesome the paradox was.

"Yes, the hotel. I checked myself in that day and have kept an eye on you ever since."

She pulled in a deep breath. "The chrysanthemums, Master?"

"How could I resist?" I tugged her hair. "You told me what you wanted."

"I didn't realize you were paying attention, Master."

"Then you don't know me very well, little girl." Finally succumbing to the call, I pressed my lips to hers, sliding my tongue into her willing wet mouth. The groan she offered ratcheted up my arousal tenfold. "But you will," I promised, forcing myself to draw away. "You'll learn when I discover something, I never forget it."

"I believe you, Master."

"I knew there was only one way to approach you again." I paused, considering not telling her about the hidden camera in the vase, but I pushed the thought away. Full disclosure was what I had vowed, and that was what I'd offer. She would know exactly how I'd found her. "The flowers were an obvious choice, and they offered me another way into your world."

"What do you mean?" Concern glinted in her gorgeous eyes.

"I mean, the vase they delivered to your room had more than one job." My pulse sped up as the admission neared. I was excited. I wanted to tell her, to see her reaction.

"It did?"

"As well as holding your blooms, it also gifted me the perfect place for my camera."

"Camera?" Her voice quivered. "You mean you were watching me again?"

"Today, yes." I watched her responses carefully. "I could see the view from the vase."

"B-But why, master?" She tried to withdraw, but my fingers held her in place.

"Isn't it obvious, beautiful?" I wanted to laugh at the distress flickering in her gaze. "I wanted to see you. I *always* want to see you."

"But…" Her words dried up as her brow creased. "I thought we'd left all that behind at the house."

"Why?" I inquired. "I never discussed the cameras except to infer how much I enjoyed them."

"It's such an invasion of privacy, Master." Her hurt was apparent in her tone as she grappled for the right words.

"Your privacy is mine to invade," I reminded her. "Just because the authorities intervened, you never stopped being mine. You had to know I was looking for you, little girl, and that I would find you."

"I…" Her hand rose to her temple, and for the first time, I appreciated that she hadn't contemplated the inevitable outcome. "I didn't know where you were."

"You know now." There was no remorse in my tone. I wasn't sorry for tracking her and had no contrition about watching her reactions. The woman was mine, and if she hadn't understood what that meant, she might as well know now. Tiffany knew I'd been in her life for months, living in her house, but I had the sense she still didn't comprehend its true meaning. She was mine, and no force on Earth could change that.

"You know how much you mean to me."

A flicker of fear flashed in her blue eyes, the first I'd seen since she'd entered the suite.

"Little girl." My digits stiffened in her wonderful mane of hair. "Do you know how much?"

"I-I didn't, Master."

I couldn't believe it was true.

"But you do now?" My mouth grazed hers as I waited on her answer. "Tell me you know."

"Yes, Master." Her voice was breathless. "I know now."

CHAPTER 21: TIFFANY

Staring into his gaze, I couldn't quite fathom his words, but his intent was more than clear, coming over in potent waves. Kade was a hunter, and I had been his prey for so long, he'd lost track of how to target anyone else. There was only me, and his sights were laser-focused.

"There's my good girl." His serious expression faded into the powerful smile that subdued my other senses. "I knew you'd understand."

Understand? Frankly, I was still reeling. The fact he'd been watching me yet again, as recently as when I'd returned to my room, was chilling. Presumably, that was how he'd known I'd returned, how he knew when to message. God, he'd watched me receive those messages and seen my responses. Even after everything we'd talked about, he still thought it was acceptable to behave that way.

"Master..." My throat seemed to close, warning me to carefully consider my next words.

"Hmmm?" He tugged me closer, pressing me against his chest.

I breathed in his earthy male scent. What was it about his smell that was so damn alluring? Why did my head cloud? Why did my hips want to rock back to meet his throbbing cock?

"Will you always watch me?" There, I'd said it. I'd voiced the primal fear bubbling in my chest.

"Watch you?" He sniggered as if there was something amusing about the question. "There'll be no need, little girl. We'll be together."

Always? He couldn't be serious. "What about when we're not together, Master? What then?"

Kade's huge palms landed on my shoulders, pushing me a few inches away. "What's all this?" His brow creased. "Why won't we be together?"

"Well." My mind raced, trying to quell my rising panic and vocalize a coherent answer. However frightening his possessive streak was, this version of Kade was a hundred times better than the man who'd bound and tormented me in my house. I was rueful to upset him. "There will be times you're in another room somewhere." I shrugged, attempting to look nonchalant. "Will you have cameras rigged to watch me?"

For one protracted moment that seemed to go on forever, Kade stared, his hands holding me in place as he contemplated my scenario. I held my breath, fearful of even taking in air until I knew his verdict. Would he find my suggestion funny, or would it rile him?

Eventually, as though he understood the effect the delay was having on me, the corners of his mouth curled. Relief flooded my system.

"Master?" I could hardly even force the word out.

"I'm sure I can trust you in another room, can't I?" He leaned closer, his mouth nuzzling my nape.

"Yes, of course." I swallowed, reveling in the feeling of his lips as they worshipped my sensitive skin.

"Of course, what, little girl?"

I tensed at his cautionary tone. "Master."

"Mmmm." He sounded unimpressed. "I haven't had to prompt you for a while." His face lifted to meet mine, his smoldering expression searing into me. "Need a reminder?"

"Master?"

He was doing it to me again, blazing through my needs and rational senses with nothing more than a lingering look and a few well-chosen words. Once again, I was reminded I'd never known a man like Kade, never met anyone with his conceited audacity. I'd never come close to knowing someone who could so easily set me on fire. It was an impossible quandary I could never square in my head. How could I want him so badly yet be overwhelmed? How could those two emotions ever marry?

"Need me to remind you who your master is?"

His smile grew, suggesting he had already decided, and his question was irrelevant. Perhaps this was Kade's attempt at democracy, the new third way we had decided to try, but if it was, its veneer was thin. I could already sense his mind was made up. I was owed that reminder, no matter what I said.

"What kind of reminder, Master?"

The query was my last-ditch shot at reasserting some authority into the situation, but I didn't know why I bothered. The final fragments of my influence had fallen away as soon as I was stripped and brought to heel—a place I had been more than happy to fall into—and it was too late to complain.

"The kind that sees you upturned over my knee." The dark twinkle in his gaze had returned, and my heart hammered in unbidden response.

"A spanking?" I gasped, conscious of how my clit throbbed at the promise.

"That's right." He grinned, pushing against me. "It's been too long since your bottom was reddened."

Fuck, he was right. It had been way too long.

"Yes, Master."

"We agree that's what you need?" His gaze widened, daring me to defy him.

"Yes." I nibbled my lower lip. "Will you go easy on me, Master?"

"You're asking me for mercy?" Kade laughed dryly. "After all the trouble you've caused?"

"I just…" Hesitating, I assessed his face, trying to discern if he was serious. "I haven't been spanked much, and the last time you swatted me, I was sore for days."

"Little girl,"—his voice had taken on that soothing quality—"It sounds as if we need to train that little ass of yours."

I shifted on his lap, acutely aware of just how naked and vulnerable I was.

"There'll be lots of spanking in your foreseeable future. For one thing, it's a good way to correct your behavior," he went on. "For another, it's just a lot of bloody fun."

I swallowed at the glee in his voice. My nerves were falling and rising in waves I couldn't control, but I didn't deny the reality—the sound of the spankings was far more enticing than it should have been.

"That should help your tolerance for my palm." He smiled, simplifying everything in that Kade-like way he always did.

"You want to spank me now, Master?" My gaze flitted around, although I didn't know what I expected to see. By now, I knew the lounge in his suite and had discovered its corners.

"Yes." He eyed me intently. "But I want your consensus."

Consensus? My brows knitted as my heart raced. This truly was a first.

"Tell me you want it." His gaze burned into me. "That you need and deserve it."

"Oh God." I heaved in a breath, lightheaded as if standing on the edge of a high building. "Master, please."

"Or tell me you don't." He drew away a fraction. "Explain to me how it's of no interest, and you don't merit it."

My gaze fell between us. I couldn't say that because it wasn't true. I wanted the spanking, and maybe, after the way I'd sliced his throat, I deserved it, but anxiety still rippled. Could I bear it? Would it be sexy and consuming, or would Kade's palm be intolerable?

"Little girl?" His deeper tone prompted me to respond.

"Please spank me, Master." I lifted my head to meet his gaze, my focus falling over his scar as I confessed. "I warrant it."

His hand rose, tilting my chin back toward him. "You deserve it." His voice was serious. "And you want it. Don't you?"

"Yes, Master." I nodded, ensnared by the dark gleam in his eyes.

"Say it."

"I want it." I scarcely recognized my voice. "I want you to spank me."

Time stretched out as he held me there, suspended by the thumb and forefinger that had captured my jaw. Then, as if someone had just hit fast-forward, he rose to his feet, taking me with him, and carried me to the opposite sofa.

Clinging to him, I couldn't catch my breath as he lowered, forcing my feet to the carpet on his right side. I panted as he settled, waiting for the inevitable hand signal to tell me when to move. It came just as I couldn't take anymore, his index finger pointing to his lap.

"Down."

Our eyes met, and the intensity propelled my feet. Folding over his lap, my fingertips grazed the carpet on one side as I rose on my toes on the other. Closing my eyes, I waited for my nerves to rise, intensifying until they overpowered, but as I pulled air through my nostrils, I realized it wasn't apprehension that riveted me. It was arousal that stirred in my core, swelling until it was difficult to focus on anything except the pursuit of his hand as it skimmed my skin.

"I'm so pleased to have you back, little girl." His palm brushed my lower back, settling on my prone and exposed backside. "Back where you belong."

"Yes, Master."

"At first, I thought you'd orchestrated the police's disturbance because you didn't want to be mine." He squeezed my left butt cheek. "It hurt to think that."

"I'm sorry."

Kade had changed track, his voice taking on that edgier quality I'd learned to fear. It wasn't dread that filled my senses but eagerness. I wanted him to do it, lift his palm and strike me. I longed to hear the impact as the sting resonated, craved the closeness I knew it could bring. More than that, I had to know—was this desire to be spanked real or just a creation I had conjured in my daydreams? Was it something tangible I could use to heighten and empower my pleasure? Kade had crashed into my existence and awoken my senses, and I was finally able to see how it could benefit me.

"I had time to think." His fingers slipped between the cleft of my ass cheeks. "Time to realize you were only overawed."

My breaths were ragged as his fingertips skimmed my rectum.

"You weren't rejecting me. You just needed time."

Oh God, why didn't he just do it? I'd asked him to spank me. What was he waiting for?

"Isn't that right, little girl?"

"Yes, Master." Hell, I could hardly process his words.

"That's right." His digits paused over my labia, taunting me with the pleasure we both knew they could deliver. "You've had that time now. Time to realize this is darkness you cannot fight, and neither should you try."

I curled my toes into the carpet, willing my body to be still as he toyed with me. That's what he was doing—what Kade always did—tormenting until I couldn't take any more before he struck.

"Master." I sounded pained, although he hadn't even swatted me yet.

"Hmmm?"

I could definitely hear the glee in his answer.

"Please," I murmured. "Please just—"

I never finished my sentence. His palm vanished in an instant, reconnecting with my upturned ass a few seconds later, and he didn't hold back. The spank rang out as the hurt ignited. My lips parted, releasing the energy his delay had created in one loud yelp.

"Is this what you wanted?" he growled, striking me again.

Fuck. Yes, this was what I wanted. "Yes, Master." I cringed as a flurry of fast, insistent swats landed, robbing me of breath.

"Good." Over and over, he spanked, peppering my ass with hard, unrelenting smacks. "Then you get what you want, little girl."

Targeting each part of my ass, Kade ensured every inch of

me was tanned by his palm, lowering his hand to connect with my frantic pussy every few swats. I cried out with the pain but was duly ignored, his rhythm unhindered by my reaction.

"Take it, little girl." His words were a low snarl. "Take what you chose and what you are given."

Balling my hands into fists, I grappled for composure. I had yearned for this—had asked for it. It was too late to plead for mercy, but Christ, how had I forgotten the power of his strikes? My backside must be almost twice its usual size, and his pace conveyed little desire to pause.

"My little girl will be spanked whenever she displeases me."

I groaned at the thought, tensing as he struck the sensitive underside of my cheek.

"Whenever she disobeys or deserves punishment."

Fuck, I couldn't take much more. When I'd sought the spanking, I'd only envisioned a few intentionally targeted smacks to exaggerate my fervor, but I should have known better. Kade wasn't the kind of man who delivered playful spankings. He was the type who hid in my attic, waiting to strike.

"Fuck." I choked out the word after a particularly painful impact.

"Language, little girl." He didn't hesitate, switching his attention to my vulnerable sex. "There'll be more spanks unless you control that mouth."

"Yes, Master."

My voice was hoarse as he spanked my pussy, my hips rising to accept more. Brows knitting, I acknowledged that however much the onslaught hurt, my body betrayed my true feelings, my clit tingling with need and seeking more punishment.

"What's this?" He laughed, sending the next bout of spanks against my sex. "Does my little girl like her penance?"

"Yes." There was no point denying it. "Oh God, Master!"

"You. Are. Per. Fect." He punctuated with a fresh strike, each blistering a different part of my pussy.

"Oh!" I gasped, arching my back to receive more of his palm's focus. Something switched in my head, the precipice where the offensive tipped from pain into bold, burgeoning pleasure. This was the part I craved, the reason I was prepared to submit and suffer through the torment.

"Tiffany." For the first time, his arousal was obvious in his raspy tone, audible even over the sound of the relentless smacks.

Oh God. My eyes squeezed closed as the pace increased, and leaning back into each impact, I reveled in the pure sensation. It was deliciously naughty to be sprawled over him, naked and obedient. It was one thing to be compelled into compliance by his ropes and ill intent, but this was something quite different. I was there because I'd chosen to be, stretched over him because I'd requested the punishment, and perilously close to orgasm because I sought the sting of his palm.

"Master." Urgency radiated from my tone. "Please."

"Are you going to come, little girl?

"Yes." Nothing in my life had ever seemed more certain than the beautiful, rhythmic surety of his striking hand. "Yes, please."

"You're incredible."

My muscles tensed at his smug tone, and I held my breath as the spanks rained down, catching my glistening sex and desperate clit. I hoped to all that was holy he wouldn't tease, wouldn't take me right to the edge and deny me. Hanging off the cliff by my fingernails, there was nothing I could do to resist. I was entirely at Kade's mercy.

"Do you know how long I have waited for a cumslut who comes apart at the strike of my palm?" His voice echoed over my head from some distant place, a goading impetus to my already amplifying ardor.

"Mas…" I couldn't manage the whole title, my head clouding with the pleasure.

"Come then." He chuckled, intensifying the pace of his strikes. "Come for me."

Lost to the frenzied passion, I called out as my desire peaked, heat boiling in my core as every muscle in my body stiffened at the moment of climax. In that one blissful moment of joy, I flew, unable to take a breath or think, only exist and revel in the absolute glory of the feeling. Grabbing the carpet, I bit down on the hedonism as wave upon wave of satisfaction pounded me.

"Beautiful," he purred, spanking me lightly while my body spasmed.

"Master." The title had real meaning. No other man had ever owned my body like this. Kade was its maestro. I groaned as his palm finally paused, and two fingers brushed my swollen labia before delving into my sex.

"Your cunt is wonderful," he praised, pushing deeper.

Panting with need, my hips rose, silently inviting him to take more of me.

"Fuck, you're wet."

I smiled as he vocalized what I was thinking, thankful he couldn't witness my blushing embarrassment. No matter how hard I reconciled my desires, shame always surfaced at the idea of finding pleasure this way. Biting my lip, I realized shame was part of what I craved. I'd buried my passion for so long, it bubbled up in bizarre and unusual ways. Under

Kade's tutelage, it was the mortification that pushed me over the edge.

"Yes, Master."

"I want you." Withdrawing his fingers from my pussy, he smacked my ass cheek as he ushered me from his lap.

I collapsed over the edge of the sofa on my knees, and my hands gripped the leather as he rose behind me. Inhaling at the sound of his zipper, I bit back on my grin. This was exactly what I needed.

"Stand up," he ordered. "Face down and ass in the air."

I rose on shaky legs, absurdly vulnerable yet never more aroused.

"Good girl." His crown nudged my entrance as he once more swatted my tender ass cheek. "Now, you get to be useful again."

CHAPTER 22: KADE

My senses erupted as I buried my prick in her warm, wet cunt. Clenching around me, she groaned as I withdrew and slammed back inside. I'd missed this—this sense of oneness and intimacy—every inch as much as I'd craved the carnality. Filling her was the most natural feeling in the world, and pounding her hard over the couch, I realized I would never tire of our connection.

Tiffany was my world, and this visceral pull between us was its very center. However gratifying I'd imagined taking her would be, I could never have envisioned a lust as powerful as this.

"Fuck, little girl."

I gripped her hip, steadying myself as she pushed her face into the seat and moaned for more. The woman was clearly made for me. With only limited training, she'd accepted her role and relished it.

It didn't matter that we were screwing without protection again, that I could very well impregnate her. I should have cared, for her sake and mine, but God help me, the sense of delight was so great, all I could rationalize was the pleasure.

"Fuck."

Pulling away before I toppled over the edge, I blew out a breath. Much more of that stimulation, this would all be over, and I wanted it to last for as long as it could. We both deserved that much.

"Master?" She glanced back at me with frantic blue eyes, and that's when it hit me. There was still a part of Tiffany I had yet to claim, and this moment—our first union after she'd willingly walked back into my life—was the perfect time to take it.

"Stay." I pointed to her, then turned and lowered my pants before kicking them from my ankles. She gripped the edge of the sofa cushion as I shifted the coffee table away, almost spilling the remaining wine. Moving back to her, I fell to my knees, spreading her tempting ass cheeks with my palms.

"Master?" Panic gripped her plea, but it was met with a sharp swat to her upturned backside.

"Settle." My warning resounded as my cock throbbed with new urgency. It liked what I saw and approved of my plan. "I'm going to devour you."

Splaying her wider, I didn't wait for permission. Pressing her face into the leather, I buried myself between her legs, lapping at her pussy and spreading her copious arousal north. Tiffany tasted wonderful, the most intoxicating cocktail I'd ever indulged in. By the time I rose from her delicacy, dragging a finger from her soaking sex to her ass, she was groaning with need.

"Oh, Master." She sounded hysterical. "More… please."

"Not this time." I chuckled at her greed. "You've had your pleasure, and now, I get mine."

Plunging a finger into her ass, she clenched around it as

she let out a string of indecipherable noises. I pushed a second digit in place, stretching her as I enjoyed the exquisite sensations.

"Relax," I cautioned. "It's time you were mastered properly."

"B-But..." Her tone was laced with the trembling terror she'd gifted me at the house—a sound I hadn't heard for days.

"I don't want to hear it, little girl." I slapped her cheek hard as I pumped my fingers in and out of her tight hole. "This ass belongs to me, just like every other part of you." I sensed the moment she ceded, her protest wilting to a mewl as her hands splayed on the leather by her face.

"Better."

Pulling from her, I delved back between her cheeks, adding more than enough lubrication to aid my intent. Rising, my balls tightened, my erection swollen and desperate for relief. It was time I sought my own satiation. Climbing up, I hooked one foot on the sofa and angled my crown against her sphincter.

"Breathe," I encouraged, pressing forward. I watched her taking huge mouthfuls of air, deliberately slowing her intake. On her next exhalation, I lunged, slipping a couple inches past her tight ring of muscle.

"Fuuuck." She clutched the couch, her head rising as if she intended to wriggle free. Steadying her shoulder with one hand, I pressed her forward as I eased back, then pressed deeper.

"What did I say about language, little girl?"

That was an unfair criticism. Tiffany could hardly think, let alone keep her vocabulary in check, but I couldn't help myself. It was heavenly to goad her, and inching inside her tight passage, the hedonism was almost too much to bear.

"I-I'm sorry," she stammered, clenching around me. "My God."

I had to agree. I'd rarely known decadence like it.

"Don't move," I barked, trying to process the pleasure as I withdrew, only to reclaim her again.

"Master!" she panted.

"I'm not hurting you," I reassured, thrusting as gently as I could. "Now, do your job and concede."

Whatever remaining fight had lurked inside her slipped away, her eyes closing as she caught her lower lip between her teeth.

"Better," I praised, moving a little faster.

I wouldn't be able to last long like this, but fucking her ass was so deeply tantalizing, I didn't care. I owned all of her holes and would take them whenever it suited me. Tiffany would learn there would only be satisfaction for her when she succumbed without a fuss. I held her orgasms in my hands, just as I possessed every other part of her being.

Leaning over her, I pressed my palms into the seat beside hers, sliding into her ass with slow, deliberate lunges. My balls contracted, the sensation nearly painful as my climax loomed.

"Yes!" Cocooning her body, I buried myself as deep as I could as I filled her ass with my seed. She cried out into the leather, then turned to catch my eyes as I roared with consummation. Lodged in her tightening passage, I folded over her and grunted into her hair as another round of passion consumed me.

"Master." Her tiny hand shifted, and the feeling of her skin brushing over my outstretched fingers roused me from her sweet-smelling hair.

Smiling, I watched as she placed her palm over mine.

Raising my hand, I lifted hers to my lips, planting a kiss on her knuckles.

"Now, little girl," I told her, nudging farther into her claimed ass. "Now you're truly mine."

CHAPTER 23: TIFFANY

Writhing in my seat, I glanced at the man in the driver's seat. It had been two weeks since Kade had ruptured my boring existence into a world of submission and indulgence at my request, and in that time, he had been true to his word.

We remained holed up in his suite for days, avoiding messages from Detective Lucas while I negotiated with Rex for more leave. My boss was perplexed at my sudden reluctance to return, but given the relevant sketchy details about the ordeal at the house, he was forced to accept my need. The company owed me enough holiday to take the entire month, so Rex had little choice but to assent. It bought us another fortnight before I needed to go back—time Kade intended to use to his advantage.

Smuggling me out of the hotel under cover of night, he moved us to a guesthouse under false identities before hiring a car and driving north. That was the car I was sitting in, watching the light fade as he zoomed along the highway.

"What is it, little girl?" He didn't turn to meet my stare but could no doubt feel the weight of it. "Something you need to say?"

My brows knitted at his taunting question, my teeth tightening around the huge ball gag he'd secured into my mouth before we'd left. Kade was well aware I couldn't reply properly. He was also conscious of how damn horny it made me.

"No?" He chuckled wryly. "Too hot, maybe?" Reaching forward, he redirected the flow of air to me, channeling it straight at my exposed chest.

"Oooh," I complained, squirming harder in place.

It was one thing to be gagged for the journey, but Kade had ensured the entire trip was a blur of aroused tension. Having acquired new toys online while we were still hotel based, he used the new purchases to scintillating effect. The shiny new butt plug was in my backside, while the cruel new clamps bit down on my nipples. To add to my humiliation, I was stripped, with my arms bound behind me. Finally, my ankles were forced apart by the spreader bar he'd bought. An echo of the night I'd first encountered him, the spreader bar ensured I couldn't close my legs or fend off his advances.

"There." He tugged at the small metal chain that connected the nipple clamps, and I groaned as the additions pinched harder. "Is that better?"

"Od." Throwing my head back, I looked at the roof of the car, wondering how much more I could take before I burst into flames.

We'd settled into something of a twisted routine at the hotel, with Kade's will becoming my universe. It was ironic. I'd once studied law, intending to make sure its rule was upheld throughout the land, but these days, the only laws that mattered were the ones he laid down for me. His long list of requirements revolved around two main precepts—his pleasure and my obedience. Closing my eyes, I recalled all the incredible carnal adventures we'd undertaken in such a short period, and one facet remained true. Since the day I'd walked into his suite, however hard he pushed me, he always touched base with me about our dynamic.

Night after night, after having used me as his footrest, insisted I kiss his feet, or fucked me into submission, he ended the intensity in the same way. Pulling me into his arms, he whispered the same six words into my ear.

How are you doing, little girl?

It was the one opportunity I had to explain how serving him affected me, to tell him about the commands that veered close to the line, and seek solace for the acts we'd shared. That one change had shifted everything between us. Now, I had an outlet—a time when I could speak without fear of reprimand and a daily dose of the reassurance I needed after hours of his relentless orders. It had become the lynchpin of our relationship.

Ignoring the bite of the clamps as the cold air attacked my breasts, my brow furrowed. *Relationship?* Was that what this was? Pulling in air through my nostrils, I acknowledged the latest trail of saliva as it slid from the ball down my chin. Yes, this was a relationship. It wasn't founded in any normal social conventions, but it was special and unlike anything I'd known. I didn't hope to rationalize all the things I felt or try to map out where we'd go when I returned to work. Kade had made it clear—he would take care of those things—and gave me enough other matters to contend with in the meantime.

One thing was for sure. The more time I spent with the man and the more I ceded control, the less I cared to reverse my decision. I'd walked back into his life with my eyes open, searching for the one thing I'd never been able to find—a man who could tend to all my needs. I'd had no idea that very man was lurking in the shadows of my life, but now that I'd discovered him, I was falling deeper and deeper under his spell.

"You make me so hard." He laughed, shaking his head as he accelerated.

Due to the way Kade wanted me to travel, we'd had to wait until the end of the day to leave the guesthouse and had many miles to drive before we reached the mysterious destination he had in mind. Naturally, he'd refused to tell me anything, peppering my ass with spanks when I'd dared to ask more. Sighing, I relaxed against the seat as far as my binds, clamps, and plug would allow. Suspended in a state of constant arousal, I had learned Kade had multiple ways to control my behavior, and despite my protests, every one of them ignited me.

"Need some relief, little girl?"

Rolling my head in his direction, I caught the twinkle in his eyes despite the fading light.

"Es, Aster." I had little hope he'd allow me to come, but perhaps he'd take pity on me and remove the clamps while he drove.

"My beautiful whore." His hand slid straight between my legs.

Groaning, I tipped my hips toward it, thankful for this touch. He slipped his fingers between my lips, whistling at the inevitable arousal he found.

"My, my, little girl. Soaking, as ever."

I wasn't mortified at the accusation anymore. In fact, perverse pride surfaced at his words.

"I bet it wouldn't take much for you to come." His lips curled, though his focus was still on the road. "Only a few minutes grinding that greedy clit against my hand, and you'd explode."

I mewled, frantic for the release he'd described. Kade hadn't let me come all day and most of the one before, though that hadn't prevented him from playing with me and ratcheting up my excitement. The repercussions for climaxing without his consent were higher than I wanted to risk while we were traveling, so I'd worked hard to abide by his rules, but increasingly, I couldn't think because of my arousal. The man was most definitely a sadist, and I fucking loved it.

"Go on then." His chuckle encircled me as he dipped his hand, slipping one fingertip inside my quivering sex. "You have my permission, but you only have the next five miles." He gestured ahead to the road. "If you can rub yourself to orgasm before we pass Grantham, you can come."

I gasped around the gag, my hips already swirling into action as they pressed closer to the source of the sweet friction.

"God, you're wonderful." His laugh deepened. "If only I could record you gyrating like a bitch in heat, but it's okay. I have enough hours of recordings of you degrading yourself to last a lifetime, with a lifetime of chances to make more."

Heat furled at his disquieting words, no doubt intended to strengthen my desire, and they worked just as he'd hoped. Sliding down the seat, past the safety belt, I splayed my thighs as I rocked my hips. I knew what I must look like as I succumbed to his nefarious plan, but I didn't care. Denigrating myself was all part of the deal, and Kade was there to make sure I never had an easy ride.

"Three and a half miles left, little girl." Glee emanated from his voice. "Don't you want to come?"

Lifting his hand, the fingers in my pussy tweaked my

throbbing clit. I cried out around the gag, conscious of the sudden hurt morphing into slick need.

"Es, Aster."

"Then come on," he taunted. "There's only about three miles left."

His hand slid back into place, and I ground against it like a demented animal. Gagged and unable to move my hands, I had no choice but to obey, my desperation for pleasure more pressing than anything else. Each gyration dislodged the butt plug shoved in my ass, the sensation reminding me of the times Kade had fucked me there. I was certain that was the point. He'd told me often enough, when he wasn't claiming the hole, it was his to plug.

"Less than two miles…"

I tensed at his smug tone. "Oo od."

I was close, so close to erupting around the plug and over his palm.

"Just as well I put you on a towel, little girl," Kade sniggered. "You're making such a mess all over that seat. Maybe next time, I should find a pet carrier and keep you caged in the back."

My breaths were frantic as I imagined the scenario.

"Naturally, you'd be gagged, bound, and plugged," he went on. "But at least you wouldn't leave wet patches everywhere."

Stiffening, my thighs captured his hand as the idea of the dehumanizing treatment bounced around my head. I could easily see Kade following through with the threat, and the worst of it was, I suspected I'd bloody love it.

"Aster!" I called his name as the rush of hedonism stole my breath, my head slamming back against the car headrest. Rubbing me gently, Kade smiled as I whimpered. I rode the waves until I could think straight again.

"Good girl." He slid his hand away, examining my juices in the half-light. "And with only half a mile left as well."

Slumping against the seat, I moaned around the gag, "nk ou, Aster."

"You're welcome." He reached for me, and expecting an approving caress, I leaned toward his hand. Watching in horror, I saw him yank one, then the second clamp from my nipples. Hurt burst through my satiated serenity. "That's better." Dropping the clamps onto the seat between his legs, he smirked. "Now you can get some sleep without me worrying about those beautiful tits."

"Eep?"

"Yes." He glanced in my direction. "We have hours. I suggest you close your eyes and rest. You have no idea what I have in store once we arrive at our holiday home."

CHAPTER 24: KADE

Carrying her into the cabin, her head rolled to my chest as I took her weight. Living with my little girl and bleeding pleasure from her gorgeous body while demanding she service my needs had been everything I'd hoped for and more. Now we had the chance to indulge ourselves in this secluded place for two weeks. I couldn't fucking wait.

"Master?" She turned her face to me, her eyes flicking open.

I adored how the word was the first thing from her lips these days when I removed her gag as if it was the most natural address in the world.

"Hmmm?"

"Have we arrived?"

"We have," I confirmed as she lifted her head and gazed around at the interior. "It's late, and it's dark. We'll explore in the morning." Placing her on her feet on one of the oversized rugs, I helped her to her knees. "Wait there while I get the bags."

She exhaled, folding over her thighs though her hands were still loosely bound behind her.

"Will you be okay?"

Her weariness gave me pause for thought, my feet halting as I watched her.

"Yes." Her voice was little more than a sigh. "I'm fine, Master. Just tired."

That was hardly surprising. I had kept her on the edge for days, only permitting her release in manners that titillated me. Tiffany's head must have been in a near-constant fog of arousal.

"I won't be long," I promised, already striding out and down the steps to collect our things from the car.

Our unorthodox genesis meant we didn't own many possessions, so there wasn't a great deal to bring inside. Tiffany couldn't return home without arousing suspicion from the police, and I was keeping a low profile for obvious reasons. Locking the car, I was once again grateful for online deliveries. Without them, we'd have struggled to survive.

By the time I made my way inside, closing the door behind me, Tiffany had edged toward an easy chair, leaning against it for support.

"Hey." Dropping the bags, I paced in her direction and crouched beside her. "You're not tired, little girl. You're exhausted." A pang of guilt echoed in my chest. The day she'd walked back into my life, she'd given herself over to me, which meant her health and welfare were my responsibility. I'd spent too much time reveling in my power and not enough energy focusing on her needs. That needed to change while we were at the cabin.

"Maybe." She managed a small smile as I tugged on her binds, releasing the ropes at her wrists. Rubbing her skin, I lowered her hand to her thigh.

"Come on." I gestured to the doorway ahead. "There's a bedroom over there. Let's get you settled."

"Not without you, Master."

One weary hand rose to my chin, grasping at my stubble, an act I would never normally have permitted, but something about the adoration in her eyes ensured I allowed it. Tiffany had come so far in such a short space of time, and I couldn't be prouder of her progress. For reasons only she knew, she had put her trust in me—the monster who'd stalked her nightmares and captured her—and even with the compromises I'd made, I was in little doubt which of us had taken the bigger leap of faith.

"Don't worry." I scooped her into my arms and rose to my full height. "I'm not leaving you." Stalking to the bedroom, I pushed the door open. The rising moonlight cast an ethereal pale illumination over the space, highlighting the enormous bed in the center. Moving toward it, I dropped her gently on the sheets.

"There." I pressed a kiss to her crown. "Get comfortable. I'm going to find some heat."

"You can warm me up, Master."

I glanced back at her playful tone, the edge in her voice the first sign she was well.

"I will," I assured her. "But even I get cold sometimes."

She chuckled, tugging the cover and snuggling inside. Her ankles were still forced apart by the spreader bar, but otherwise, she was unhindered as she settled.

"Stay right there." I turned in the doorway, throwing her a wink.

"I promise, Master."

Striding back into the lounge area, I flicked on a lamp and found the wood heater. It didn't take long to flood the space with heat, the pile of already chopped wood ensuring we'd be warm for some days to come. Rising from the heater, I wandered to the refrigerator, collecting a chilled bottle of water and some fresh fruit before returning to the bedroom. Feeling for the light switch, I watched as Tiffany turned away from the sudden illumination.

"Here." I smiled, finding her exactly where I'd left her. Walking to her bedside, I collected the waiting clean glass and placed down my spoils. Opening the bottle, I poured her a glass before handing it to her. "Drink."

"Thank you, Master." Her lips twitched as she took it. "I am thirsty."

"I'll do better at catering to your needs while we're here," I vowed, perching on the edge of the bed.

"*All* of my needs, Master?" Her voice had taken on a raspy quality, conveying the particular types of need she was referring to.

I laughed at the lust dancing in her beautiful eyes.

"The ones pertaining to your health and wellbeing," I clarified, offering her an apple. "The rest will depend on your behavior."

"As I suspected." She met my gaze, biting her lip. "I try to be good."

"You're bloody amazing." A sudden surge of sentiment rose, reminding me just how lucky I was. After everything I'd done, I had no right to call a woman as wonderful as Tiffany my own. She should be far out of my reach, but there she was, compliant and ready to give me everything. I was one lucky son-of-a-bitch. "I don't tell you enough."

"Master?"

Her brow rose, sensing the subtle shift in my tone. God only knew Tiffany was so aligned with me, she could probably tell what I was thinking without having to ask. That was the reality of the time we'd shared since our forced separation. Depraved and absurdly intimate, Tiffany had become the other half of me—the better half.

"I mean it." Pulling in a breath, I tugged her toward me. "I'm one lucky bastard to have you."

"Actually, you kinda just took me, Master." Her tone was sardonic, another indication of how comfortable she'd become in my company in recent days.

"And then you came back to me," I reminded her wryly.

"Yeah." She shrugged. "I guess I'm just crazy."

"You're nothing of the sort," I chastised, standing to pull my shirt over my head. "You're completely sane, little girl."

"Are you sure?" She smiled, her gaze drinking in my torso as I rounded the bed to my side. "Would a normal woman choose to be treated this way?"

"Screw normal," I replied, unfastening my belt and pushing my pants to the floor. Kicking them away, I climbed into bed beside her. "Who wants that mundane shit?"

"Evidently not us, Master." She glanced down at the glass in her hand.

"That's right, and I'm not sorry." I watched her fingers tighten around the drink, my mind fleetingly returning to the night she'd pulled a knife on me.

As if Tiffany read my mind, her brow furrowed. "I am sorry about that, Master."

"What?" I asked, feigning ignorance.

"Hurting you." She motioned toward the scar on my neck.

"I know," I answered. "You told me, and as I recall, we *dealt* with the matter."

She fidgeted on the bed. "I know, but I just wanted to say so again."

"I wasn't exactly putting your needs first then." I chuckled, aware that was something of an understatement. "I don't approve of your violence, but I understand, little girl."

"Are you putting my needs first now, Master?"

"That's a bold question, little girl." I shook my head at her sarcastic tone, pinching her nearest nipple until she yelped. "Would you like to rephrase?"

"I just meant I have needs you're not meeting," she cried, squirming at my side.

"I just promised to be more attentive to them," I clarified. "But sometimes, you need a reminder about who your master is, and the best way is denial."

Tiffany blew out a breath. "If you say so, Master."

"I do." I grinned, leaning toward her. "I get to decide when you come, don't I?"

Her gaze darted to her hands. "Yes, Master."

"And why is that?" I loved to remind her of our dynamic as if the bondage and gags weren't enough of an aide-mémoire.

"You make the rules, Master."

I imagined how wet the admission was making her, my cock stirring at the alluring prospect. She was always so wet for me because I knew every single one of her buttons.

"A little louder, baby." Reaching for her chin, I compelled her focus to me. "I didn't hear you."

"You make the rules." Her face burned with mortification. "Master."

"You got it, little girl." I swooped, offering her an unforgiving kiss. "I make the rules, and don't you forget it."

CHAPTER 25: TIFFANY

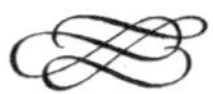

My life was almost unrecognizable.

Once upon a time, Tiffany had been a hard-working lawyer. Often overlooked by her boss, she convinced herself she was respected and that all her effort would pay off. Maybe one day, it still would, but all that effort had come at a price—her life. That version of Tiffany was all work and no play. She'd rejected invitations and had all but lost track of friendships—all in pursuit of her career. She was a strung-out, uptight insomniac who saw things in the shadows.

Except she hadn't been hallucinating, had she?

Those things in the gloom, the noises from the attic... had been real. They'd been Kade, and once unleashed, he had rained hellfire on the world she'd known. Unapologetic and raw, Kade had brought Tiffany to her knees, sculpting a woman the original version would have barely known. This version of Tiffany was acquiescent and needy. She thought less about legal cases and more about how to satisfy her master and impress him to earn her own pleasure. Lost in cascading hedonism, it was increasingly difficult for this Tiffany to think of anything but Kade.

Both women were me, facets of who I was. Both were

potential chances for the future, but as I stared into his gray eyes, only one presented a route to gratification—only one would demand he grant me what I deserved.

I make the rules and don't you forget it.

His words pinballed around my head.

"Understand?"

"Yes, Master," I answered, acutely aware that I did. It was scary to think how far down the rabbit hole I'd fallen, how badly I needed Kade in order to get through the next hour, let alone the next day. I couldn't remember how the old version of me had got by with her take-outs and self-love, but as dangerously close to the brink as I was, I never wanted to go back to that lonely place. I was much happier being with him, denigrating myself for him, willing to risk the most precious thing I had to give—my heart.

"Good." He gestured to the drink still in my hand. "Finish up and put the glass down."

Draining the remaining liquid, I placed the glass on the nightstand, along with the apple he'd thrust into my hand. Hunger had taken second fiddle to the other appetite he awakened. My heart sped up as I glanced back at him, the dark glint in his gaze conveying his carnal intent.

"We need to sleep."

I heard the instruction from his lips, though the passion blazing in his eyes begged to differ.

"Yes, Master."

I was dog-tired but couldn't deny the way my clit throbbed. Kade lit me up in ways I couldn't fathom, and even the slightest gleam in his eyes had the power to transform me from drowsy to excited in record time.

I was falling for him. I knew I was. I watched my love-sick reactions as if I was a stranger eyeing a car crash in slow motion. It was clear what was about to happen—I'd witnessed every lurid event—but there was nothing I could do to prevent the inevitable. If I wasn't already head over heels for Kade, completely helpless to prevent his provocation, I soon would be. He'd said I could return to work and transition into a world that incorporated both my own passions and my consuming desire for him. That was my future.

Groaning as he rolled on top of me, I was conscious of the reality. Kade made the rules. Sprawled beneath him, I had little inclination to revolt. It was true what they said—true love really was suicide. I was willing to give up everything to never lose this feeling.

"Soon, we'll talk about what comes next." He pulled me down flush at his side as he rolled onto his back.

"Master?" Rolling toward him, my fingertips skimmed the soft hair on his chest. Christ, Kade was gorgeous and even sexier now that he'd revealed his softer side. Sure, I was attracted to his predatory dominance, but sometimes, it was good to know he was human. "What do you mean?"

"Your return to work." His jaw clenched.

"Oh." My pulse quickened. Had he changed his mind about permitting me to work, and if so, what did that mean? Was my career a hill I was willing to die on? After so many years, it certainly should have been, but… was it?

"No need to sound so downbeat." He glanced in my direction. "Nothing has changed. You'll still be working."

"Okay…" What was that in my voice… disappointment? "What do you mean then, Master?"

"I mean, what hours you'll be allowed to work." His lips curled. "And what you'll wear when you do."

My brows knitted. No one had ever held me to account on either of those issues, and as stupid as it seemed, I had the impression neither would be as simple as they sounded.

"You'll tell me what to wear?"

"Of course." His smile grew. "Not just your work attire but also explicit instructions about what underwear you're permitted, and..." His voice trailed away, the silence blooming around me into terror.

"And?" I croaked.

"And I'll find some training harnesses for you. Something to remind you whose whore you are, even when you're playing the hotshot lawyer."

Fuck. The muscles at the apex of my thighs all clenched at the same time.

"What kind of harnesses, Master?"

"I told you." He rolled away, still grinning, though the impressive tent in the covers below conveyed his thoughts on the idea. "We'll talk about it soon. For now, you should rest."

Blowing out a breath, I tried to think past the most recent mist of arousal his words had inspired.

"Can I freshen up before we sleep, Master?"

It was ridiculous how horny it made me to have to ask for his permission to use the bathroom. In the beginning, the thought had been harrowing, but now, it was only impetus for more desire. Kade had the Midas touch—everything he did stimulated me.

"Yes, little girl," he replied. "But first, there's something you can help me with."

His hand shifted over the covers, stroking the outline of his impressive erection, and my gaze followed, torn between my yearning to feel him inside me again and my longing to unwind and rest.

"How can I help, Master?" In the end, the passion won out —always the passion.

"Climb on top of me." Flinging back the sheets to reveal

his hard shaft, he gestured for me to comply.

"But Master,"—I sucked my lower lip past my teeth at the look of his thick organ—"I still have the spreader bar."

"Did I ask you to delay?" His tone had lowered, spiking my heart rate.

"N-No," I flustered, already sitting upright.

"Then why aren't you on top of me?" His eyebrow rose. "I want you on my cock."

Heart racing, I maneuvered into position. Kade's ankles drifted apart as I hovered over his cock. Lifting his legs, his feet slipped over the metal bar separating mine, effectively pinning me down while he guided me over his crown.

"Down." Only one word, but the order sent an exhilarated thrill through me, and slowly, I eased over his shaft.

Fuck. My eyes fluttered closed as I accepted all of him, his cock even bigger because my ass was still filled with the plug he'd shoved there earlier.

"Ride it," he commanded. My eyes flew open when his hands grabbed my breasts, squeezing them as I moved. Shifting to my nipples, he pinched the tender tissue, smirking at my squeal. "Faster."

Rocking my hips backward and forward, I increased my pace, electrified that, even though I was theoretically on top, Kade was still the one calling the shots. His hips rose to claim me at the same time I rode his hard length, my burgeoning climax already fueled by the endless tantalizing ways he'd teased me throughout the day.

"Hands behind your head," he growled, his eyes darkening as I obeyed.

Forcing them into place, my lips parted as my hips kept the pace.

"Good. Now, tell me, whose tits are these?" Shaking my nipples, a shot of pain morphed into hot, slick arousal.

"Yours, Master." I was so fucking turned on, I could scarcely articulate what he wanted to hear. "They're yours."

"And that cunt?" he went on, driving hard into my needy sex. "Who does that belong to?"

"Y-You," I stammered, absurdly exposed and vulnerable, even though my hands were untethered.

"What about that full ass?" He leered, reaching around to swat my backside. The strike reverberated to my core, and I clenched around him in response. "Is this mine, cumslut?"

"Yes, Master." God, I was so close to coming apart. "It's all yours."

"Good, little girl." He chuckled. "You're gonna ride me until you've milked all the cum from my cock, then you're going to climb off and make sure your cunt caught it all."

Oh, Lord.

"And what will you use to clean my cock if any has been missed?"

"My mouth, Master." I rocked myself closer to hedonism, painfully aware he hadn't even mentioned my pleasure.

"Good." His smirk grew. "Are you close, little girl?"

"Yes, Master." My reply was immediate. "I'm so close."

"You're not here for your own satisfaction." Reaching for my breast, he tweaked my nipples until I cried out. "But if you come by the time you've milked and cleaned up my cock, so be it."

Thank God. I let go of the breath I hadn't even known I'd been holding.

"Yes, Master. Thank you."

"Don't forget what you're here for, though." His dark eyebrow arched. "*My* pleasure."

"Y-Yes, Master." I gasped, my back arching as the first shoots of my orgasm rained over me. "I w-won't forget."

Laurel Turner was the first life I extinguished—a switch that flipped in my head and sent me on a killing spree that lasted for years. It had taken Tiffany Noble to set me free—a woman who could engage as well as gratify.

Seeing her stretched out on the bed, a sense of repletion washed over me. She was the woman who had liberated me from the vicious cycle of destruction I'd been locked in. Enslaving Tiffany had been a fantasy I'd played out in my head a hundred times before I ever laid hands on her, but the reality had a more potent side-effect.

She had set me free.

Reaching for her ankles, I released the spreader bar from one, then the other limb. Tiffany was fast asleep, exhausted after our latest sexual marathon, but she curled into a ball in response, drawing her gorgeous legs away from me. I smiled as she settled, pulling the cover over her ravishing body.

The urge to nurture as well as annihilate was new to me, but looming over her resting form, I found I rather liked the challenge. It was easy to devastate. I was a master at it. It was something else, though, to cherish and cultivate. Like the orchids, that was the need Tiffany inspired in me and one of the reasons I was falling for her.

Walking back to the lounge area, I lowered the light in the bedroom and collected our bags as that thought played out in my head. I *was* falling for her, and if I didn't know better, she was starting to feel the same way about me.

Love was indeed a crazy emotion—unlike any I'd ever known. I'd conquered fear and learned how to manage loathing, but love had eluded me until now. It had been conjured in the midst of my darkness and obsession, and despite my every attempt to obliterate Tiffany's freedom, crush her spirit, and even her own attack on me, the sentiment had grown in those murky shadows. Pausing at the dining table, I glanced back at the bedroom door. There were no words to say what a feeling that strong could achieve, no limits to what I'd do to keep her, to never lose that sparkle in her eyes when she looked at me.

I would do anything, give anything.

It's because she doesn't know.

My brows knitted at the uninvited voice in my head. Its analysis might have been true, but it was still unwelcome.

That's why she looks at you that way, why she's falling for you —she doesn't know who you really are.

My hands balled into fists, my heart pounding as I turned and headed toward the kitchen area. It was true. Tiffany didn't know who I was. Even though I had learned a great deal about her, she only had a handful of nuggets of information about me.

"I'll tell her," I whispered, wanting to scream them but conscious she was sleeping next door. "I'll tell her everything."

Then she'll hate you. When you tell her, you'll wreck everything you've salvaged from the house, the police, and the hotel. It will be over.

"No." My tone was clipped as I pulled back a chair and collapsed onto it. "I'll never let her go."

An unexpected well of emotion surged, taking my breath away as my hands gripped the table. Having never been in love, the swell of emotion was new. For the first time, I had something to lose, someone I was prepared to sacrifice myself for rather than see her demise. It was an ironic viewpoint from the man who'd overseen the end for so many others, and the sardonicism wasn't lost on me.

"Don't worry, little girl." My fingers relaxed their grasp on the wooden table. "I won't let anything happen. I'd rather twist myself in knots than give this up."

It doesn't matter! It won't make any difference, you moron. The moment she discovers who you are, she'll leave.

"I won't let her," I mumbled.

You won't have a choice.

My back straightened at its surety.

She'll find a way. Just like she did before.

Memories of the knife she'd used to assault me flooded into my mind's eye, bleeding into my recollection of the way she'd contacted the police. Tiffany had a proven track record of throwing a spanner in the works when it suited her.

"No." Jaw clenching, I pushed the distorted memories away. "That won't happen again. Things are different now. We're different."

Deep inside, I truly believed it. The way she looked at me had altered—the longing in her eyes was tangible and not only related to the lust I inspired. Hell, even the way it felt when we fucked was different. There was a tenderness in her touch, a longing I hadn't acknowledged before. Tiffany had changed me. She would understand. She had to understand.

You're dreaming. You're always fucking dreaming. You can't expect her to stay when she discovers the truth. The best thing you can do is keep quiet. Say nothing about your past. Let her believe you're nothing more than a regular guy.

I rose from the chair, my heart hammering with frustrated fury.

"I can't." I raised my voice, wincing as I realized how loud it had become. "I can't carry on like this. If we're going to be together, if this has any chance, I have to tell her. I have to be honest."

"Tell me what, Master?"

Spinning at the sound of her voice, panic exploded as my gaze landed on my beautiful nymph. Without her binds, she'd made her way to the doorway, brow creasing as she wrapped the blanket around her.

"Little girl." I fought hard to regain my composure. "What are you doing there? You should be sleeping."

"I woke and heard you." She tilted her head as she continued. "I thought there was someone else here? It sounded like you were having a conversation."

"No," I answered, frantically replaying the one-man show she'd just witnessed in my head. "Only me."

"Oh." Tiffany's gaze darted around. "Then who were you talking to, Master?" She stepped closer. "What do you have to tell me?"

Time stood still as I watched her move, protracted seconds where I considered defaulting to form and denying any knowledge of the things I'd said. I could lie and tell her the *she* in question wasn't her or morph into her master and insist she had no right to quiz me.

I did none of these things.

"Come here, little girl." Beckoning to her, I encouraged her toward me. I could hardly believe the words as they fell from my lips, but then that was the Tiffany effect. Everything was different, including me.

"We need to talk."

The End.

Devour *Enthralled By The Darkness for* the next sizzling installment of Tiffany and Kade!

Read the introduction to the book now...

ENTHRALLED BY THE DARKNESS

Prologue: Tiffany Noble

Sweet black silence. The type I once avoided with blaring televisions and constant noise now offered solace. Breathing in, I stretched out on the comfortable surface, rolling and searching for him, my master—Kade. The scent of him lingered on the sheets, but as my hand searched the space beside me, he was nowhere to be found.

Eyes flickering open at the disconcerting reality, I eased myself upright, concentrating on the question rattling through my head. Where was he? Where was the man who'd exploded into my life, changed everything, and brought me to this cabin in the middle of nowhere?

Pulling in a deep breath, I blinked into the shadows. What the hell had happened to me that I sought the comfort of his touch? I'd been intimidated by Kade, petrified even, but now I craved his attention.

I'm falling for him.

The answer burst into my head as if it was so obvious, I should have known it innately, and on some level, I did. For days, I'd been sliding into deeper and more meaningful feelings for the man. Since I'd walked into his suite, something had altered, and my emotions had become entrenched. I looked to Kade to offer me the darkness I'd always been too afraid to follow. I was attracted to his danger. Even though I didn't know where this road would lead, I sensed it was the right path—the one that would give me peace of mind, as well as satisfaction.

"No."

I tensed at Kade's clipped tone, his voice floating in through the open doorway, followed by the noise of a chair being dragged against the wooden floor.

"I'll never let her go."

Brow furrowing at his words, I slipped from the sheets, grabbing at the top blanket and wrapping it around me. Moving quietly across the rug, I held my breath as he spoke again.

"Don't worry, little girl." Kade's voice was impassioned as if he was justifying himself, but that didn't seem like Kade. The man I knew was self-assured and didn't take no for an answer. "I won't let anything happen. I'd rather twist myself in knots than give this up."

Throat drying at the solemnity in his tone, I inched closer

to the doorway, pausing again as I deciphered his next mumbled words.

"I won't let her."

"Kade?"

His whispered name was barely heard over the sound of my pounding heartbeat. Something was wrong; it had to be. Either he was having a conversation with an invisible guest who I couldn't hear, or he was talking to himself. I inhaled at the idea. Was he mad? I mean, I'd known Kade skirted the line of insanity, but this was something else.

"No." His tone was emphatic. Leaning around the door frame, I saw the resolve in his gray eyes. "That won't happen again. Things are different now. We're different."

Who the hell was he talking to, and what was he talking about? Kade had referred to a female on more than one occasion, and as far as I knew, there was only one woman in his life—me. Dread surfaced as I watched him, noting the tension in his jaw as he mused on whatever conundrum agitated him. I gasped as he rose suddenly from the table, covering the sound with the palm of my hand.

"I can't." I jumped at the volume of his voice. "I can't carry on like this. If we're going to be together, if this has any chance, I have to tell her. I have to be honest."

Enough was enough. I had to speak, had to come forward and let him know I was there, that everything was okay. We were together now. It was my job to console as well as concede.

"Tell me what, Master?"

He turned, his eyes wide and unsure. "Little girl. What are you doing there? You should be sleeping."

"I woke and heard you." I wanted to go to him, but something about his stunned expression told me to hang back. "I thought there was someone else here. It sounded like you were having a conversation."

"No." His reply was instantaneous. "Only me."

"Oh." I glanced around the lounge space, trying to calm my fraying nerves. "Then who were you talking to, Master?" I couldn't accept that he was having a conversation with himself. He seemed so irate. "What do you have to tell me?"

Using all my courage, I compelled my feet forward, closing the distance between us until his hand rose, one finger urging me even closer.

"Come here, little girl." Tension eased from his shoulders as his lips stretched into a lazy smile.

"We need to talk."

Devour the conclusion:
https://books2read.com/u/3y1L7J

Stay in touch with Felicity's new releases by subscribing to her mailing list.

FOLLOW ME!

Stay in touch with Felicity's new releases by <u>subscribing to her mailing list.</u>
https://felicitybrandonwrites.com/newsletter/
You'll also receive FREE reads just for signing up!

Love Dark Romance?

Discover ALL The Dark Necessities **universe!**
https://books2read.com/u/mdGvJd

<u>**Devour Tempted for FREE:**</u>
https://books2read.com/u/b5kPPA

Join Felicity's Facebook group, **and Discord group, to engage with her and other awesome readers!**